Anyone here seen Kelly?

Books by Linda Mann

The Tavistock Mystery Series

Mist

The Tidemaster

The Corsican Trap

Anyone here seen Kelly?

The Mr Boots Series

Mr Boots

Others

The Chronicles of Edwin Snipe

The Homicidal Publisher's Tale

Anyone here seen Kelly?

LINDA MANN

Priory Press

Published by Priory Press Ltd
The Priory, Abbots Way, Abbotswood,
Ballasalla, Isle of Man IM9 3EQ
www.priory-press.co.uk

First published 2013

ISBN 978 0 9574914 0 3

Edited and typeset by
Frances Hackeson Freelance Publishing Services,
Brinscall, Lancs
Printed in Great Britain by
Bell and Bain Ltd, Glasgow

To my mother Sylvia with much love

Linda Mann started off writing poetry and plays for young people when her own children were growing up, branching out into novels and skits for radio. She set up Priory Press in 2006 with her husband Timothy to self-publish her own books and now has over twenty writers beavering away in various garrets across the UK.

Linda is a keen performer and supporter of the written word and apart from the odd stint on local radio and treading the boards in various theatres around the Island, runs a performance group of fellow thespians and radio presenters called 'Voices'.

Acknowledgements

With many thanks to Jacqui Jones without whom this book would never have been finished.

To Frances Hackeson for sorting out all the errors and to James and Henry for prowling the Island for that perfect cover shot. To David and Chan Cook for providing the perfect writers retreat, Boatman's Cottage. To all those that nagged until it was completed and last of all to Timothy, Emma, Henry and Lucy for putting up with me and my characters for another year.

Chapter 1

Julius Wilson looked around his bank's boardroom and as no one appeared to have anything more on their mind, other than the tinkly sound of newly minted money being spent, smiled and announced that the meeting was over. Picking up the phone which always accompanied him everywhere, Julius punched in a few numbers and asked his PA to send in the caterers.

There was a brief hiatus as chairs were pushed back and bottles were opened, a vast selection of carefully prepared canapés were passed around the large boardroom with its panoramic views of London City airport and the Thames, wine glasses were clinked in good humour and the board of Wilson, Hansard and DeLouche Investments gave up any thought of doing anything useful or indeed profitable for the rest of the day.

The board consisted of Julius Wilson, their newly appointed Chairman, Oliver Mandrake, Chas Winston, Izobelle Du Maurier, Rupert Arnott Hansard, Lydia Spike and Ivan Dmitrievich Levin.

Julius Wilson was tall, well-dressed and had the face and mien of a particularly unpleasant weasel, a fact which had, at no time, hindered his rise from barrow boy and small-time crook to London investment banker. He owned a substantial quantity of low-grade rental property and a large and airy apartment in Belgravia. He was unmarried and unattached, a state of affairs which suited him as his predilection for married women was almost legendary in the wine bars and select clubs that he tended to frequent. His fellow board members were, it had to be said, a little afraid of him due in part to his acid tongue and in another to a mind which had all the warmth and humanity of a steel abacus.

Oliver Mandrake, Olly to his friends and family, was the complete opposite. Of medium height and build he spread charm and warmth as he moved around the room. He ran the offshore arm of the investment house and lived and worked on the Isle of Man, commuting once or twice a week to London with various reports. Married for the third time to a much younger version of his first and second wives, he had five children, three horses, a pony, four dogs and a six-seater private plane.

Chas Winston had been his assistant when Oliver had worked for a year or so in New York and although apparently close, Chas had never quite felt welcome once he had applied and got the job at Wilson, Hansard. Chas was a brash, likeable Harvard graduate who owed much to both his father's trust fund and his mother's model good looks. Unmarried but happily living with his partner Brian, Chas was certain that one day all that Oliver Mandrake had would be his.

Izobelle Du Maurier had originally run a rival Channel Islands firm in Jersey and was one of only two women on the board. She was clever, blonde, a qualified Jersey advocate and although possessed of cover-girl looks had not slept her way to the top as had many of her rivals including her fellow board member Rupert.

Rupert Arnott Hansard was the last of the Hansards, an old banking family which went back to the coffee houses of Charles II. Brought up mostly by a selection of au pairs and nannies while one or other parent was either abroad or in rehab, Rupert was in equal measure greedy, amoral and lazy. His only redeeming feature was a peculiar ability to pick successful emergent companies, a trait he had discovered quite by accident when working in South East Asia. He had also discovered and bought his first netsuke there, a carved ivory figure of a rat playing a small drum. Netsuke, wine and women with a penchant for PVC and bondage were his life interests; the ability to make money was to him just a means to an end and so he attended each board meeting reluctantly and almost always with a hangover.

Lydia Spike, the only other woman on the board, was a hardworking single mother of a nine-year-old boy whom no one ever saw or met. As she had also never been seen out with any man the other board members privately wondered if her young son's father had been a test tube. Lydia was bright and rather boring; she was also to the astonishment of her fellow board members completely teetotal and a vegan, both of which were regarded with universal suspicion.

The last member of the board was Ivan Dmitrievich Levin, a Russian-born banker and vodka manufacturer. Ivan spoke six languages and had two degrees, one in mathematics and the other in applied chemistry. Ivan lived in a rather grand apartment in the old MI6 building in Portman Square, something that never failed to amuse him as his father had, for most of his working life, worked for a rival secret service in Leningrad.

The meeting over, Lydia and Izobelle stood at the window nibbling on very thin sticks of celery and bitching about Ivan's latest stunning assistant.

Rupert leant against the wall and tried to listen in, while at the same time paying lip service to Chas who had imbibed rather too freely of the champagne and brandy cocktails on an empty stomach and was attempting to get anyone to listen to his ever increasing gripes about Oliver Mandrake and the Manx office.

Oliver, who had been chatting to Julius and Ivan about an investment in China turned and glared at his former employee as the whine in Chas's voice carried across the room.

"I mean it's laughable … a small rock in the middle of the Irish Sea having a space programme and Oliver wants to invest in it? Where are the rocks I ask? Eh? In his head?"

"Leave it," Julius hissed as Oliver made to move towards Chas.

Rupert, sensing that Chas had finally gone too far, smiled sweetly and taking several caviar and smoked salmon blinis from the plate Chas had begun to wave around, turned and called out to the other members.

"Well what do you know – salmon to rival anything Scotland can produce and to my certain knowledge cured and packed on a rock in the Irish Sea. Another successful Manx venture to rival that of mobile phones, which may I remind you Chas, have been pioneered over there, as was radar during the Second World War. Small, you see, but beautifully well informed."

Chas looked momentarily taken aback as both Julius and Oliver clapped and both Izobelle and Lydia cried "Hear, hear, for the mouse that roared."

The atmosphere in the room lightened, dark-clad waiters and waitresses again plied their many trays of small eats and Chas sank onto a solitary chair and gloomily watched flights taking off from the nearby airport as his colleagues progressively got merrier.

The sound of cheerful raised voices carried out into the glass enclosed hallway and writhed in almost erotic ecstasy with the aroma of hot roasted meats, spices and the sharp tang of champagne and brandy.

The lift door at the end of the hallway opened to disgorge its one occupant clutching a small dark document wallet. He sniffed the air and scowled, puritanical roots which went back to the *Mayflower* almost made him consider turning back to his neat and tidy desk. He also had a cold, one which despite the copious use of Lemsip, cough linctus and other chemicals hailed as the way to beat the germ by numerous glossy pharmaceuticals, still hadn't taken any notice of the 'please vacate the premises' notes that his body was valiantly leaving around.

A braying voice could be distinctly heard above the hubbub.

"Here's to another year and in particular The Bank of England Act 1998. God bless our parliament of owls!"

There was a clatter of plates, spoons and glass and a large rotund figure hove into view.

"Martin!" The figure cried. "Come and join in the celebration, dividends all round and we won't be forgetting you. Come payday an extra thousand or so will be sitting waiting for you to take it and paint the town red."

"Um ... actually Mr Mandrake I need to talk to you about the American figures."

Martin looked down at the wallet he was clutching and then as he felt another sneeze coming on hunted around in his suit pocket for a dry tissue. Finding none he tried desperately not to breathe. His companion hastily handed him a neatly laundered cotton handkerchief in a striking shade of magenta and Martin gratefully buried his dripping nose in it.

"Shouldn't you be at home in bed?" Oliver Mandrake

asked, stepping away from him hastily.

"I need you to look at the last report."

"What last report?"

"Exactly my point," Martin muttered. "There wasn't one, not a proper one. In fact it was almost exactly the same as the previous one and after two years of apparent building it shouldn't have been. And also I can't get hold of the person who signed it off."

"Well I can see that you'd want to clarify but the figures are where we want them to be and …"

"But …"

"Look Martin, old chap. I can plainly see that what you need to do is to go home. No, don't try to say anything. You have a stinker of a cold which we will all probably now get and then pass on to the nearest and dearest, and although I can understand how you might want to put this in front of the board, now really is not the time." Oliver glanced back to the room he had left and then with a slight frown turned back to the trembling accountant. "What I'll do is this. I'll take the report back to my office and get Clarissa to contact the American office and I'll also send a copy on to every member. But frankly if I put this in front of them now they'll discard it out of hand."

"I see." Martin looked first at his boss and then down at the wallet. Reluctantly he handed it over and with a last backward glance shuffled to the lift and on the cusp of another loud sneeze allowed the door to close behind him.

Oliver Mandrake opened the wallet and after glancing through its many pages sighed and then after a brief internal debate walked back into the boardroom, picked up another glass of champagne from a waiting caterer and stalked off towards the wide window at the back of the room, where two of his fellow board members were munching on miniature roast beef-filled Yorkshire puddings and Parma ham-wrapped asparagus.

“Oi – leave a little one for me!” he laughed, approaching the large and almost empty platter that they had between them.

“Olly, thought you’d gone to ring the better half.”

“Got ambushed by Martin from accounts.”

“Oh?”

“Some report he’s been working himself up over. Poor man has an absolute stinker of a cold, so sent him home with a promise that we’d look into it.”

His companions looked down at the papers in his hand and shrugged.

“Anyway I’ll just …” Oliver Mandrake turned, and on spotting a friendlier face, deposited the papers on a side table and hurried off with a cry of “Izobelle – how was Paris?”

Conversation ebbed and flowed around the room as the champagne bottles emptied. Another dividend, another company bought up, its loans reassigned and sold on. A successful and productive day all round.

Finally the caterers found themselves alone to wash the last glass and clear the last plate. In a solitary waste bin amongst a detritus of paper napkins, unfinished food, cocktail sticks and soggy pastry one of the cleaners came across a sheath of closely typed papers. He looked at it briefly and then with a shrug emptied the lot into a large black plastic refuse sack.

Chapter 2

Tavistock Allan surveyed the small group huddled around her and switched on her most sincere smile. She had just read from her latest book and now it was the question and answer session, something which she looked forward to and dreaded in almost equal measure. Although even she had to admit that the current audience shouldn't, on the face of it, be too hard to handle or fend off. The audience spread about the bookshop consisted of two elderly couples, a middle-aged man and his small dog, a young couple who had wandered in out of the rain and now found it difficult to leave, what looked like a trio of hardened fans on the grounds that they were all clutching at least one other past book apart from her latest, and a couple of suits clutching takeaway polystyrene cups from which the aroma of fresh coffee was wafting.

"Do you write from life?" asked the middle-aged man. His dog gave a strange whimper and then as everyone glanced at his master, yawned widely, exposing huge yellowing teeth and a large, very pink tongue and immediately went back to sleep. The man, looking slightly embarrassed, muttered, "Ignore him, he doesn't read."

The audience as one laughed out loud and Tavistock, praying silently to whoever happened to have been paying attention upstairs, grinned; a warmed-up audience and she hadn't had to say a thing.

"Sometimes," she paused and then added, "actually most writers do. The ones whose books you open and you are instantly transported to, say, ancient Rome or a planet carried on the back of a giant turtle."

"But that's not …" the man began.

"Real life. I know, it's fiction but because it's so real, especially the characters, you believe it. You see what we fiction writers do is, we take a little bit of reality and stretch it with a lot of imagination into something which could happen somewhere. So most of my characters could be real, a lot of them are a combination of real people but never one actual person … after all considering what I write, it's safer."

"Has anybody tried to sue you thinking that you were writing about them?" one of her hardened fans asked.

"No, not yet." There was a ripple of laughter. "But I have had calls from people confused because they couldn't find particular places or murder sites."

"Really? And what did you say?"

"That really depends on the site. Sometimes I admit to making it up, but at others, well if there is somewhere near that is spot on, I direct them there, especially as half the fun of reading a murder mystery is often spotting the places in the book. Like going around Edinburgh on an Inspector Rebus Tour."

"Where do you get your ideas from?" another of the fan club asked, as her friends nodded their approval of the question and then waited anxiously for the reply.

"Um … from anything really. An article in a newspaper, a story you hear in a pub, a conversation on a train or in a coffee shop. Anything really that you can say 'but what if?' to."

"I see."

"And do you just work on one book at a time?" someone at the back asked.

"No, usually I'm working on three or even four."

"How?"

"Well, I'm usually in the process of editing one, writing the current offence against good literature and thinking and researching another one or two. I think most writers do. We all have ideas our editors and or publishers either hate or don't think will sell, which is often worse. And so we keep busy, keep the little grey cells always on the hop so to speak."

"So what are you in the process of researching now?"

"Well I've got two in the cerebral pipeline, as it were. One is a Victorian-style murder mystery about Jack the Ripper set in the theatre and the other is a present-day thriller about a political sociopath who loses his place in Government and leaves to run a seaside B&B."

The suit clutching the polystyrene coffee cup raised a hand and when he had caught her attention coughed in an embarrassed way.

"Er – surely a lot has already been written about the Ripper? I mean there's that new book out by Patricia Cornwall and ..."

"Actually it's an old one she wrote some years ago and updated."

"Really? Oh."

"Yes really, and no, before anyone asks, I haven't read it. I find that if you read anything similar to what you are yourself involved in, it tends to colour your own writing. A sort of literary osmosis."

A hand shot up from the back again and waved ominously.

"So you'd do all that research and still not be able to write a book about it?"

Tavistock stretched to see the questioner but he was hidden by a large poster and only a shirtsleeve was visible. Tavistock suddenly sensed something, a feeling of menace, a cold shiver down the back of the neck. Mentally she pulled herself together and, affixing a fresh and eager smile to her face, answered.

"Unfortunately yes, but research is never really wasted; at some point, even years later you come across something and you find that it's just what you needed for a particular plot. Ah, I can see my editor waving and looking pointedly at her watch. Just one more question and then I'll be available to sign a few books and if you still have something you want to discuss I'm always happy to talk to people afterwards. Yes, young lady?"

The female half of the young couple nervously cleared her throat as she lowered her hand.

"Well, I just wanted to ask what you would do if you hadn't have found a publisher?"

"I think I would have done what a lot of writers still do … keep writing … it's something I just *do* regardless of whether someone reads it."

"So you have manuscripts that no one has ever published?"

"Oh yes. I think every author has that pet idea or book that they love and nobody wants to get into print because it's not their usual thing. Bit like the ugly child who hides in the corner desperate to be loved – and yes – before you ask, sometimes years down the line they become the literary equivalent of the swan."

The young girl suddenly smiled and then, clutching the arm of her young man looked directly into Tavistock's eyes and muttered a thank you.

The bookshop owner who had done the – to Tavistock's

mind – overly lengthy introductions stepped onto the small podium and grabbing the hand mike from the stand upon which it had been temporarily attached firmly stated, “Well I’m afraid that really is it. Tavistock Allan will now sign copies of her latest book and, as she’s said, have a more informal chat in our coffee shop located on the floor above. With homemade cakes available.”

Tavistock made her way from the podium to the table at which she was to sign and again felt that someone was watching her, someone who didn’t have her own interests at heart, someone who was very definitely walking on the dark side. But however much she looked and observed she couldn’t for the life of her work out who it could be. And then just as swiftly as it had come the feeling went, leaving her in a mild state of disquiet.

Some time later when all the books that hadn’t been signed and the bookshop didn’t want to keep had been packed away her editor cornered her as she was just about to enjoy a solitary black Americano and a large plain scone with butter.

“Ah good, there you are,” she muttered, looking around to see who may have been listening. Seeing that there was no one within hearing distance she sat and bit her lip.

“Okay Charley, out with it,” Tavistock demanded, knowing by the lip biting and general nervousness that it couldn’t be good.

“I took your ideas for both books to the board and …”

“And?”

“They didn’t like either of them.”

“What!”

“Apparently Jack has been done to death, another three are due out next week on the coat-tails of la Cornwall and the other idea McBride appears to have pinched … not the B&B … he’s set it in a care home but the political nutjob is more or less the same."

"Oh bugger Bride," Tavistock groaned, biting into her scone.

"Nice thought," Charley muttered, grinning. "So do you have any other ideas knocking about in that steel trap you call a brain?"

"No. But I'm sure I'll come up with something – after all I've still got to check out of the hotel, collect my car, drive up to Birkenhead and catch the ferry back and there will be bound to be something or someone there," Tavistock advised her.

Charley patted her on the shoulder as she rose from her chair and then happily wandered off. She had dropped the bomb and now could do no more. Tavistock briefly wondered about changing publishers, but as it had taken her nearly ten years to find her current batch of idiots and they were still in business she realised that she really had no other option but to start again from scratch.

A little later she found herself standing outside a small London auction House and decided on the spur of the moment to go in; the fact that it had started to bucket down and she had neither umbrella or raincoat and the nearest tube station wasn't even visible hastened her decision.

Inside a fairly accurate cross-section of the population sat around on a variety of old and new sofas, chairs and in one case a bright red velvet-covered chaise longue watching a rotund and cheerful bearded auctioneer wielding a gavel and peering at the screen of a nearby computer.

Tavistock watched as a variety of tat and genuine antiques were sold to a string of interested bidders. The antiques appeared to be bought by a group of three main bidders and a few buyers who even to Tavistock's untutored eye appeared to have paid well over the odds. The tat went to a variety of younger people who may or may not have been students and a rather hairy middle-aged woman who smelt.

It was halfway through the afternoon; the rain had stopped drumming on the corrugated plastic roof above their heads and Tavistock had decided to leave as everything on offer was either too big to get in her car or too expensive or just plain odd, when a box of household bits was held up. After a short hiatus the students offered up a £5 note and the malodorous bidder shook her head in dismay as an elderly gentleman at the back offered another five.

The students offered another £5 and the gentleman shook his head. It was as the gavel was going down for the second time that Tavistock stuck her hand up and waved her auction number.

"Twenty pound new bidder," the auctioneer declared.

The students gave a collective shrug and the gavel was raised again.

"Twenty pound going once, twice … sold to the lady."

Tavistock, berating herself for completely losing the plot, shuffled off to the area at the back where a young woman sat with a calculator and a cashbox and paid her already waiting invoice. Finally clutching her bulging box of mystery items she left the auction house and seeing that the rain was back and looked set to stay, hailed a taxi. Later as she threw her suitcase into the car she toyed with the idea of abandoning the box to its fate in the concrete stairwell but something stopped her as she bent to leave it by the side of the lift door and instead she moved aside a bag of shoes and her large faux fur coat and heaved it into the boot.

Chapter 3

Tavistock arrived back on the Island at an ungodly hour of the morning as her ferry from Liverpool had been cancelled due to bad weather and she'd then driven another sixty or so miles to Heysham near Lancaster and caught the 2.15a.m. sailing. Luckily there was still a cabin available so she had crawled under the crisp blue sheets and fluffy blanket supplied by the Steam Packet and promptly fallen asleep. Four hours later she awoke to find herself in Douglas and almost ready to dock according to the loud voice which had awoken her from her slumbers and was now telling all car owners to go to their respective vehicles. Blearily she got up, stumbled to the facilities and then grabbing her bag, coat and keys made for her patiently waiting little red car.

Richard greeted her upon her arrival with a large and steaming cup of fresh coffee, a warm hug and the news that he was off to the office and had a meeting afterwards. Tavistock scowled briefly but in a fairly good frame of mind watched her spouse and youngest child climb into the car and drive away along the lane.

Later that morning she hauled the auction box from the car, made herself another coffee and after carefully placing her loot on a sheet of newspaper, opened it to discover what she had actually bought.

There was a set of blue and white plates with a pattern she recognised as being one from Habitat some years ago. In fact she thought that she even had a set of eggcups somewhere in the same design. The plates were put aside to be washed later and feeling slightly less stupid she opened up the next hurriedly paper-wrapped item. It was a gold-coloured sugar bowl and milk jug. The gold was flaking and had perhaps seen somewhat better days; either that or it had always looked that bad. Tavistock gave a moue of distate and put it in a bag for the bin. A motley assortment of mismatched china followed, cheap, plain and unremarkable, but as she said to herself, the saucers would come in useful for the cat.

There followed in quick succession a bent metal thimble, a silver-painted metal model of the Eiffel Tower, a china dog with one ear missing and a hideous pink vase embellished with badly drawn roses. It had been done in the manner of the average Victorian barge painter but unfortunately with all the talent of a six-year-old with hand and eye coordination problems. Her haul around her, Tavistock sighed and got up from the floor and picked up the box. It was as she was about to toss it into the wheelie bin that the bottom collapsed and a heavily wrapped rectangle fell at her feet. Puzzled, she carefully peeled away the old newspaper to reveal a piece of tightly wound suede. Inside nestled a knife. A knife with a long ivory-coloured handle. Surprised and delighted by her find she almost ran up the stairs to her study, switched on her computer and trawled through an ancient copy of her *Miller's Antiques Handbook* until she found something that looked similar, and after another fifteen minutes of Google and Bing she found an almost perfect replica. The knife was in fact an old Victorian hunting knife complete with horn handle, probably stag. The knife sat on the papers of her desk and gently glinted in the sun.

The papers underneath were her old and abandoned notes for her Ripper story. Moving them aside she also came across all the copies of the original witness and police statements. She picked up the knife to wrap it up in its protective leather and idly wandered aloud why it had all suddenly stopped.

***

At exactly the same moment a man with a length of carefully cut rope was wondering about the same thing. Ropes and car crashes were all very well but there really was nothing better than the brisk flick of a wrist and the sudden warm spurt of arterial blood. The house he was about to enter was a large, recently updated farmhouse. An imposing and substantial home with a pristine lawn, sweeping drive and carefully tended pots in shades of blue containing a variety of black and white flowers and foliage.

Inside amongst the antique furniture and carefully placed modern items the man stopped and with almost a regretful look made his way to the side door which opened into the rear of the large double garage. It was, he thought to himself, such a pity to end it all this way. But then again he really didn't have much of a choice.

Two hours later Clara Cartwright sped up the drive, scattering small stones like shrapnel and skidded to a halt in front of the closed garage door.

"Damn that stupid man!" she shouted and hit the steering wheel.

In a thoroughly foul and evil mood she thrust the car door open and stalked to the rust-pocked garage door handle. She twisted the knob and discovered it had stuck, again.

"And you said you would fix this!" she snarled. "If I have

to go all around the house to open this, I'll bloody well swing for you, Thomas bloody Cartwright."

Clara could feel the tears of frustration, which had been building up ever since the phone call, welling up again behind her eyes. Big girls don't cry, she sniffed and then kicked the garage door hard. It moved inwards ever so slightly so she kicked it again and then as it began to swing, she shoved it with her shoulder and then pushed the metallic slab upwards. Panting with the effort she stopped and was about to congratulate herself, when she caught sight of the thing swinging gently from the overhead metal beam.

"Arghhhh!" she screamed and backed out into the summer sunshine. The body hung above a small pool of yellow liquid, surrounding a solitary leather loafer.

Clara staggered to the car and clambered in. Safely inside she fished around for her handbag and extracted her small mobile phone and dialled 999. A message flashed up and she almost threw the small rectangular object at the windscreen.

"I know it's an emergency number it's why I'm ringing it! You stupid bloody thing."

Clara held her breath as the faceless voice asked her which service she wanted.

"Police and an ambulance, Cartwright House, Upper Walpole Lane, Little Bixton, just off the M62. It's my husband. Oh my God – what if he's not dead! Surely no one could be that colour and live … hang on I'll check …" Clara erupted shakily from the car and stumbled back into the darkness of the garage.

Thomas hung bleakly above her, eyes staring unseeingly at the opposite wall, his tongue protruding from his mouth, swollen and black. Clara could feel the pent-up frustration of the preceding horrible weeks welling up inside her, tears forced their way out and she snapped.

"You stupid, stupid, stupid bloody man, what the hell did you have to do this for. Why Thomas, *why*?" And then she lashed out and hit the corpse which swung sideways and then hit her back. It was cold and flabby and most definitely dead.

Clara backed hastily away and then turned and threw up outside and all over the carefully planted black petunias in their blue glazed terracotta pots.

***

Clara spent the rest of the day answering questions, sometimes the same ones two or three times and making endless cups of tea and coffee. It was like the parish fete all over again, she thought, only with more uniforms. Part of her watched, and listened and replied and the other part of her hid and kept remembering odd and up to then unimportant things.

A night in France cowering under a large oak as the rain fell, Thomas's strong arms around her, his warm musky scent keeping her safe.

The little bistro they had found in the middle of nowhere, candles, wine and the sharp citrus tang of fresh lemons squeezed gently over a huge plate of steaming seafood.

Thomas laughing as he fell off the ladder trying to fix the Christmas lights.

And then just as the day was ending Clara remembered one final thing. She and Thomas standing at the side of their hired boat, watching the last blue fender gently floating away and then suddenly picking up speed, as it neared the waiting weir.

"Oh God Thomas, not again," she could hear herself moaning while at the time trying not to laugh.

"Clarikins pet, you know I can't tie a knot for toffee, never have and never will."

Clara sat up and gasped: it was like being hit by a large

bucket of ice-cold water. Thomas couldn't possibly have hung himself, not without help, not on his own. But the police were satisfied it was suicide; they had said so in calm soft voices of concern. He had been alone, all alone. The note was sitting on the mantelpiece in the lounge, everything neat and tidy. Nothing for her to do.

He'd been so upset about the company going into administration, about the bank foreclosing, about the staff, about her. All that worry, all that responsibility. It had all been in the letter, every last painful, desperate word. And yet he couldn't tie his own shoelaces, it's why he always wore slip-ons, why she always had to fix his tie before he left for the office.

And if they were so convinced it was suicide then she was equally convinced that it was murder.

***

There was an inquest followed by a funeral. Everyone she had ever known turned up and ate the funeral meats, drank the funeral sherry and said nice things in hushed tones about a man she still loved in her own way. When they had gone she started to pack the waiting boxes, to sort her life into crates to be shipped to her new home, bags to be dumped or boxes to be given to one deserving cause or another.

Finally with every room cleared she took her old passport out of the small shoebox in which it had been kept and held it tightly in both hands. Clara Cartwright had died, but Clara Callister still lived. She would go home. Home to the place she had been born and initially raised and then she would look up an old schoolfriend, someone who regularly dabbled in death and ask her advice.

By then she would know who had killed her Thomas.

Her lovely wonderful, infuriating, funny, irritating Thomas.

And she would ...

Her eyes rested on the carefully wrapped package at the bottom of the shoebox. Her mother had passed it on to her together with the diary and the thing in the jar. She had no daughters of her own, no children to hand it to.

"So it might as well be used," she mused, carefully unwrapping the long-bladed, horn-handled razor. It was still sharp, surprisingly so, considering how old it was.

"Well Great Gramps, your legacy lives on. And for one night only, revenge will be sweet, cold and delivered in style."

Chapter 4

Tavistock could feel the cold, she could even taste the ice in the air. Around her the silence of the place seemed to wait and was broken by the nervous cough of the man standing directly behind her.

"You disapprove, Jack?"

"It just seems a waste, that's all."

"It's winter and I doubt if she would have survived the first snow."

"I don't know much about such things but what if she's …?" The question hung in the air as the grey cold frozen fog crept down from the hills towards the loch, on whose shore they both stood. In front of them eyes bright with pain and yet dimming with death, the doe tried one last attempt to stand and failing fell heavily back onto the bracken and soft emerald-green moss.

"Pregnant?"

His companion nodded and then looked around almost fearfully.

"Let's see, shall we?"

Tavistock felt the blade go in and twist, she smelt the blood heard the fearful scream and still the blade sliced through fur and flesh and fat.

"You see, nothing."

"But we can't just leave it Sir, not like that, not here … not …"

"On his Lordship's land?"

His companion nodded uneasily.

Tavistock felt herself straighten up, wiping the knife, red and sticky with blood on a patch of grass and reeds as she did so. A clean wipe, a movement practised and fluid.

"Cover it in branches if you must, let the foxes and crows feast. I doubt if he will miss one amongst so many of the creatures. Besides it's one less mouth to feed when the snows come."

Together they turned from the blood and the sickly sweet, warm smell and walked away towards the large turreted house that could be plainly seen through the leafless trees.

Tavistock found herself whistling.

"I enjoyed that," she said, remembering the feel of ripped flesh and the shuddering jerk of the Doe's pain. "Let's do it again."

Tavistock looked down at the knife in her hand and with a scream dropped it. The smell of frost and the vista of grey water, stark branches and steep hillsides of bramble, browning bracken and humps of verdant moss faded as she woke amongst the papers strewing her desk. The hunting knife that she had been holding was released and she sat up trembling.

"You all right?" Richard asked as he stood in the doorway of her study clutching two steaming mugs, one in each hand.

"I came home but you'd gone to sleep at your desk so I thought I'd just bring you up a cup of coffee."

"Oh I'm sorry love, I just seemed to have dropped off. I haven't even been to the shops yet."

"Don't worry, Emily had a McDonalds on the way home and I wondered if you'd like to forget about cooking and go to the Abbey for dinner?"

Tavistock smiled and reached out eagerly for the coffee.

"What did I ever do to deserve you?"

"Have no idea but it must have been really good," Richard grinned, sipping his drink, before adding. "Tony was telling me that they have venison on the menu again."

Tavistock shuddered as she remembered the look in the deer's eyes as the knife went in up to the handle.

"Oh no, no venison. Not for me."

The knife lay innocently amongst her papers but as she turned to go she was sure that there was a gleam of red reflected in the dull silver-coloured blade.

Chapter 5

Oliver Mandrake stood at the window of his bedroom and watched the evening sun setting behind the far hills, a ball of orange and red the colour and size of a large blood orange, and took a mouthful of well-matured single malt.

He savoured the taste that came from spending a lot of money on a whisky produced by a small distillery nestling in the highlands and thanked his lucky stars that he no longer needed to search amongst the shelves for the cheapest heavily blended supermarket brand, which he was sure was made in a bucket in Slough.

His wife could be heard somewhere in the depths of the house shouting at someone, by the tone it was probably one of the children, and then he heard the telephone ring. After a while it was picked up and there was a short period of silence before his wife appeared in the doorway. She was still clutching the telephone and she was trembling.

Oliver, who was becoming increasingly adept at gauging how close to sobriety his wife and mother of two of his five children was, decided that it must have been a good day as she was almost sober, and moved towards her.

"What is it, Pumpkin?" he asked, all concern and worried frown.

She looked at him and then at the telephone in her hand and burst into tears.

Oliver reassessed her state and backed away a step.

"Well?" he asked, a slight edge to his voice.

She looked up at him and muttered something.

"What?" he barked.

"He said, he said I ought to ask you what you did."

"What *I* did? *Who* did?"

"The voice on the phone, he asked me if I knew what you did, how you earned the money to keep me in handbags and the children at private school. He said he knew where the bodies were buried and then it laughed. I thought it was someone from the office … it was just a voice and it …"

"It what?" Oliver despite himself felt a little afraid.

"Told me to be very careful as I could be next."

"Next?"

"Yes, I could be next."

His wife trembled and then suddenly sat on the nearest item of furniture. "But I said I didn't know what he was talking about and that you were just an investment banker and he …"

"He what?"

"He said, 'That's what you think, is it?'"

"And you?"

"I didn't say anything, I couldn't think of what to say."

"And was that it?"

"No, he said that if I didn't believe him I could ask Martin, as Martin knew all about it."

"Martin." Oliver turned and as he did his face became ever so slightly set, as if it were turning to stone.

"Martin, eh?" he repeated.

"Yes dear. Who is Martin?"

"Martin is our accountant and if he's got anything to do

with this, he's also going to be very shortly unemployed." Oliver growled, grabbing the phone and punching in his office number.

"Terry is that you? Good, go and get that weasel Martin, as I want a word. Yes I'll hold." There was a silence as they both waited for Martin to take the call. Fion looked at her perfectly manicured hands and Oliver looked at the telephone.

Eventually, after what seemed like a very long time but was in actual fact a mere minute or so, the phone trembled and let out a high-pitched trill which changed to an electronic version of *The Simpsons* theme tune.

"Have those kids been playing with the programmes again?" Oliver asked crossly as he remembered a board meeting which had been going quite well until his mobile, which he thought that he'd programmed for silent vibration, had interrupted all concerned with a loud and tinny rendition of 'Bob the Builder'. Fion shrugged and Oliver turned away from her as he concentrated all his attention on the person at the other end of the line. He listened for a minute or so said, "I see," and then switched the telephone off and sank onto the end of their emperor-sized bed.

"Olly, what did they say? Olly – say something – you're beginning to frighten me. Did you speak to Martin? Was it him?"

"Fion, love, exactly what did he, she, it, say to you at the end?"

"That I could be next."

"Right." Oliver Mandrake got up from the bed and seeing his discarded jacket put it on and hurriedly moved towards the door.

"Olly!" his wife shrieked. "What the hell did Martin say?"

"Nothing," Oliver replied with an odd glint in his eye. "He

said nothing because he's dead. That was his assistant Molly. The police had just been in contact as Martin is dead. He was killed this morning on his way into the office."

"Killed! How?" Fion gasped, her hand going hastily to her mouth.

"You know that sign that says 'Please mind the gap'?"

Fion nodded.

"Well apparently Martin didn't and he fell under the ten thirty from Sevenoaks."

"Isn't that a bit late to go into work?" his wife asked with a frown.

"Yes, yes it is and the other odd thing was that he lives nowhere near the place."

"Oh Olly, what do we do?"

"Do? We do nothing, you hear me – nothing. And now you are going to take the kids to the cinema to see that cartoon they want to watch and then you can go and stay at the Sefton with them for a few nights, while I see a man about a lot of cameras, some siren-like alarms and if necessary a very large dog."

Oliver Mandrake, on seeing his usually fluffy and bubbly wife's distress, went over to her and gave her a large hug.

"It's only for a few days, Pumpkin, I'll have the call traced and find out who it is that is making threats and then I'm going to throw the proverbial book at them or him or her. Now go and sort out the children and tell Mrs Whatsherface to go home and take a couple of days off, at least until the new security is in place."

And with that Oliver Mandrake rushed off, leaving his bemused and shaken spouse to organise the rest of the retreat.

Chapter 6

Ex-Detective Inspector and Assistant Chief Constable Bob Callow was about to leave his office when a dishevelled man barrelled into him as he was coming down the stairs and the strange man was going up.

"Oi matey, where's the fire?" Bob asked, holding his assailant well away from him.

"I have to see Bob Callow, it's a matter of life and death."

"Really? And you're sure it can't wait until tomorrow, during usual office hours?"

"No it bloody well can't!" Oliver Mandrake exploded.

Bob gave him a long hard look born of the experience of taking many witness statements and turned around and went back up the stairs to his office which he unlocked, then unset the alarm and switched the coffee machine back on.

"Want one?" he asked, indicating the basket of Tassimo products. "Only if you do, have a bit of a shifty through that lot as I have no idea what's in there."

Oliver gave a grin and selected one which Bob put in the machine after his own espresso.

"So?" Bob asked as he finally sat back down at his desk. "What can my detective agency do for you?"

"I'd like you to make sure my home is secure."

"Why?"

"Because today my wife received a very odd and threatening phone call, the information contained in part of the conversation could only have come from one member of my staff and today that staff member appears to have had an unfortunate accident."

"Ah."

"Ah is not exactly the word I would have used but it's sufficient. My wife was also told that she was to be next."

"Oh."

"I want you to set up cameras, alarms; you name it, I want it and bugger the expense."

"And what exactly do you do Mr …"

"Mandrake, Oliver Mandrake."

"Mister Mandrake, what do you do?"

"I'm an investment banker."

"I see."

"Look Mr Callow, I know that bankers in general are not well thought of, but he was threatening my wife and possibly my children, so could we have a bit less of the 'you bankers deserve anything you get expression'?"

"Sorry," Bob muttered with a grin,"it sort of slipped out."

"Apology accepted." Oliver grinned back. "After all it's an easy mistake to make. Actually there are one or two of the breed whom I could also easily bump off."

"Really?"

"So will you do it?"

"Yes. First thing tomorrow, the lads and Clive our hotshot techno nerd, will put in cameras, working on real time and attached to the office, heat sensors, sound and weight-activated sensors and a few little gizmos I would rather not talk about. By tomorrow night you will be able to ascertain if a leaf drops on your lawn."

"Good, good."

"Now I'll just take down your basic details, name, address, etc. and my tech team can get cracking."

Bob passed over a simple new client form which Oliver Mandrake completed in neat, bold capitals and then they both stood up and shook hands.

Bob then escorted Oliver to the front door and after seeing him disappear amongst the scurrying late night shoppers, went back to his office and with a sigh got hold of his partner Clive, to inform him that the match would have to be recorded, as they had new paying work that needed to be sorted out then and there.

"With a bloody great panic button in all the rooms," Bob muttered to himself as he picked up the telephone again to call his wife and ask her to take his dinner off the stove, out of the oven, or if necessary away from the dog.

Chapter 7

Tavistock opened her eyes and found herself staring at a window draped in dull red velvet. A man appeared from a doorway and she recognised him as Jack, her recent lochside companion. She was also in a large bed, a four poster piled high with stiffly starched white linen and a satin bedspread in a lurid shade of green with cherry-red poppies, worked in tiny embroidered stitches. The body that she appeared to be occupying, stretched and yawned and then yawned again.

Jack deposited the tray he was carrying on a small table by the door and then crossed the room and opened the heavy curtains with a deft hand.

"Well Jack, and how is the weather today?" she found herself asking.

"There is a light mist on the river but it bids fair to be a good day, if not a little on the warm side, Sir."

"Good. I have a lecture this morning with old Appleby and a little light and warmth always helps, not that I will be able to understand much that he says."

"Indeed, Sir."

"Now hand me my breakfast, there's a good chap."

The tray was duly retrieved and placed on the bed at Tavistock's side and she could clearly smell coffee, toast, eggs, bacon and something meaty.

"I see that you managed to procure some kidneys – excellent – and a few mushrooms too. I trust that the black pudding is from home?"

"Indeed it is Sir, and Cook kindly sent down some of her excellent marmalade and a large fruitcake."

"Wonderful."

Tavistock found herself eating a hearty breakfast while she watched Jack moving about the room. Clothes were fetched from a large wardrobe, inspected and brushed, where and when a spot of lint was found. A large ewer of steaming water was then poured into a bowl upon a dressing table set against the far wall and shaving paraphernalia was checked and cleaned when necessary. Eventually satisfied that all was in order Jack turned and asked, "Will you want to be shaved now Sir, or shall I come back with some fresh water?"

"Oh now will do, I've finished all but the last of the coffee. Is it a different brand?"

"Yes indeed Sir, Fentons have a new batch in fresh from the Americas and were anxious for your opinion."

"Well I hope you got a damn good discount, if I'm to be their guinea pig."

"Yes indeed I did sir, quite a substantial amount."

"Good."

"And may I enquire as to the taste, Sir?"

"Actually rather pleasant, sort of mellow, not as strong or as bitter as those beans you acquired last month. Buy some more if you can."

"Certainly Sir."

Tavistock climbed out of the bed, wrapping a large quilted robe about her and then went and sat at the dressing table. She was almost shocked to see that her reflection was that of a young man. A quite handsome young man, with startling blue eyes of a rare lightness. But the mouth even at such a young age seemed to her to have a petulant and spoilt downturn to it.

"You know Jack, I thought I might go to the theatre tonight, cheer myself up with a little dark relaxation." Blue eyes stared into the mirror and held the gaze of Jack's deep brown ones.

"Indeed, Sir?"

"I thought I'd go and see Mansfield at the Lyceum, get a box and hide in the corner."

"I hear that his portrayal of Dr Jekyll and Mr Hyde is without parallel; I must confess that I would have liked to have witnessed it myself," Jack murmured, covering his young master's face with shaving foam.

"Well then, you can come with me."

"Oh but ..."

"No, don't thank me, after all you can be useful procuring refreshments and ... er ... other things of interest."

Jack gave a little sigh, almost but not quite inaudible.

"What?"

"Nothing, Sir, nothing. I was just remembering the incident at the Pavilion."

"She was a mistake."

"An expensive one." Jack paused at the look that had come into his young master's eyes. "If I might be so bold, next time we may not be lucky enough to be able to find such an understanding and indeed biddable parent?"

"How was I supposed to know that the little tart was only eleven? She looked twelve."

"I hold myself entirely to blame and indeed I also thought that she was above the age of consent."

"She shouldn't have struggled so. It wasn't as if she hadn't done it before."

"According to her mother it was her first time but the father accepted a suitable sum in the end, I thought it worth it to pay the extra. Although it may be as well to steer clear of that particular theatre for some time."

"Hmmm, I suppose so." Tavistock noted that the petulant look was back and then without warning the eyes seemed to turn to ice and she found herself glaring into the brown eyes of her manservant.

"Are you trying to tell me what to do Jack? Because if you are …" The threat in the voice was clear and to Tavistock's amazement taken on board by the suddenly respectful figure who had at last finished the shaving process.

"I meant nothing Sir, nothing at all, it is just that I heard from Blanche …"

"That doxy you have back home?"

Jack frowned and for a second or two the brown eyes hardened.

"My fiancée, my wife when you have qualified and no longer require my services, leaving me to return home as already agreed by your father."

"Whatever." The young man shrugged; the status of any of his servants was unimportant to him and as he had no intention of going home also irrelevant. "Anyway what did this woman of yours say?"

"She said that your brother was in the process of arranging to come to London."

"What!"

"He has some sort of meeting or indeed string of meetings with various senior members of the clergy and is going to be staying in Westminster for a week or so. I thought that I should say something because if there was another incident and he was approached …"

A silence fell upon them as Jack carefully cleaned the razor and his master contemplated his reflection with a frown.

"The dog was a mistake," he admitted, biting his bottom lip.

"There have also been rumours."

"Rumours?"

"About your relationship with the nurse."

"What nurse?"

"Mary Jane."

"Nan?"

"Yes, Nan. Certainly enough to cause a certain amount of whispering."

"We are friends, nothing more and nothing less; she has helped me a few times. Clever little thing, knows more about medicine than the so-called doctors."

"As long as it is purely platonic."

"And where did you get that brave new word from?"

"Unfortunately I was educated, Sir."

"Pity in some respects, but no one is perfect, Jack."

"Yes indeed. And will that be all?"

"Yes for now. I'll read up on the abdomen before I get dressed just in case the old fool asks me a question."

"Very good, Sir."

"Oh – and Jack."

"Yes Sir?"

"I'll have some more of that excellent coffee and then you can go and procure us a box for tonight."

"Yes Sir."

Jack left, taking the shaving materials and bowl with him. He returned to take away the breakfast tray, reappearing a short while later with a fresh pot of coffee. Tavistock sat and stared at the anatomy books in front of her and then felt someone grab her shoulder from behind.

"What the devil do you think you are doing, Jack?" she shouted in alarm.

"Tash are you all right?" She blinked and found her husband Richard looming over her.

"Richard?"

"Yes love, it's me, Richard – your husband. I'm home late as always and demanding to be fed." Richard smiled down at her and then frowned.

"What time is it?" Tavistock asked, raising herself from the papers she had fallen asleep over at her desk.

"Nearly eight, er, who the hell is Jack?"

"Jack is … I don't know but I keep dreaming about him."

"You keep dreaming about Jack the Ripper?"

"No not him, Jack isn't the Ripper. I'm not sure why I keep …" It was then that she saw that for some reason she was clutching the knife she had bought at auction. She looked at it at the same time as Richard did.

"What the hell is that?"

"An old Victorian hunting knife I found it in that box of bits I bought at auction."

"Oh good grief, not another box." Richard closed his eyes and shuddered. "So tell me, but let me sit down first, just exactly how much did this one cost?"

"Always the accountant, eh? And before you start, it didn't cost a lot, a mere twenty pounds – less than a theatre ticket and it contained some really useful –."

"Cat dishes?"

Tavistock sat back and grinned. "Well yeah, all right it had some very useful cat dishes."

Tavistock let the knife fall onto the desk and after a brief stretch stood up and walked to the door. Richard followed after a brief glare at Tavistock's latest acquisition. In the silence that followed the blade glowed briefly red and then faded back amongst the papers and documents strewn around Tavistock's computer.

Chapter 8

Bob Callow sat in the comfortable cream leather armchair and stared at his client who sat opposite in an identical chair.

"So you see," Oliver Mandrake concluded, "I may be next."

Bob steepled his fingers and then looked up at the ceiling.

"What?" Oliver demanded.

Bob looked back and directly into his eyes; there was something not quite right, something that didn't fit, but for the life of him Bob couldn't see it.

"Look, Clive and I have put in all the security links, all the equipment and all the preventative measures we can possibly think of and there is really no way that anybody could get into this house without our knowing about it."

"Really."

"Yes, really."

"Good. Look I know that I'm being a bit heavy-handed about this but my wife and children are very important and I go away a lot. I just don't know what I would do if something happened to them."

"There is absolutely no reason to worry about them, we have surveillance installed 24/7 so ..."

"So there really is no need to worry ... but a party? Can't I just tell her to forget it?"

"Look Oliver, someone may or may not be serious but you can't live your life looking over your shoulder and your wife and children certainly can't. I mean, if we were living in say Italy or somewhere with a high level of hostage crime like the Middle East, then yes, we would be far more concerned but this is, after all, the Isle of Man – and when was the last kidnapping here?"

"I don't know, has there been one?"

"My point exactly, this is one of the most peaceful and possibly dullest places on the planet with a few possible exceptions when it comes to serious crime. So the bottom line is, I don't see why your wife's party can't go on. After all, we can have people on bouncer duty as it were and all guests have to bring their invite or be recognised by your good lady."

"But how?"

"We have her stand next to us at the front door, greeting each guest and anyone who she doesn't accept we gently take to one side and escort from the premises."

"I suppose that would be all right."

"Good. Apart from which I don't want to be the poor sod that has to inform Fion that she can't have the charity ball that she has taken nearly a year to plan. Do you?"

"Oh God no."

"Right well, if that's it, re the party, we can go through the list of people you think may have a grudge and may have rung your wife with menaces."

"Well it's not Martin, although to be fair even alive I couldn't see him threatening anyone. I can't believe that any member of my departmental staff could."

"Mr Mandrake could you just run through the list of people it might be?"

"Okay, I have here a list of everyone associated with companies that we have bought up or closed down or … well some of them and most of their employees will probably be a bit mad."

"Good God, there must be thousands here."

"Hundreds certainly."

"And the list of your co-Directors."

"Here, although I can't really see any of them … well Chas might I suppose."

"Chas?"

"Charles Winston. American, likes to be called Chas, thinks it makes him more user friendly."

"And does it?"

"Not in a month of Sundays. Nasty little beast. Found him going through my files once, when he worked as my assistant in the States. Wouldn't trust the little shit more than I could throw him. But don't think he would stoop to murder though, too much of a wimp."

"Anyone else?"

"Julius Wilson, doesn't much like me. Working-class background and an inverted snob of the first order. Then there's the Russian, very clever, well-educated, speaks several languages and would sell his own mother for sixpence. The girls are sound and Rupert is far too lazy to do anything."

"But he might tell someone else to?"

"Oh yes. God – hadn't thought of that. Hadn't thought that they might get someone else to do their dirty work." Oliver sat in a thoughtful silence for a minute while it sunk in and then uttered with a sigh. "If any of the board is behind this then frankly they could all afford to get someone to terrorise my wife. I just have no idea why."

"The report you said Martin was worried about, the one he showed you after the last board meeting."

"It's funny you should mention that. I couldn't find it after the caterers cleared up and I checked the day after with his personal assistant and it's not on the computer anywhere."

"No back-up?"

"Well if there was one, and there always is one somewhere, nobody can find it. I asked his wife to check his home computer and she said that there was nothing on that either."

"So the file died with him."

"Apparently so." Oliver frowned. "The police still say it was an accident."

"Surely there were cameras at the station?"

"Yes, but all they saw was Martin falling. There was a big crowd around him, lots of milling around and then he fell forwards and over the edge."

"Could someone have pushed him?"

"It would have to have been a pretty hard shove."

"But possible?"

"Yes, it's possible."

Bob watched as Oliver Mandrake, normally so sure of himself, bit his lip and worried at a hangnail.

"Look, I'm sure it will be all right Mr Mandrake, and really there is nothing else you can do, apart from leave the Island and go and live somewhere else."

Oliver visibly pulled himself together and stood up as Bob closed down his laptop and returned the list of suspects to his attaché case.

"Well Mr Mandrake, I'll see myself out, and don't worry, we will find the culprit. For all you know it could have been someone on any of those lists who got really drunk and decided to give you and your wife a scare out of sheer vengeful nastiness."

Oliver Mandrake nodded and forced a smile. Bob patted him briefly on the shoulder and then left. Oliver watched him leave and then as soon as he was sure that he had gone went over to the cocktail cabinet and poured himself out a very large drink.

Chapter 9

Tavistock Allan lay amongst the pillows and listened to the snores emanating from her husband. Silently she debated the rival merits of pushing him gently onto his side or kicking him but conveniently just at that moment the noise suddenly ceased. Tavistock stayed absolutely still just in case he should start again and then wondered if he had actually stopped breathing. Richard shuddered, made an odd, wheezy snuffling sound and rolled over of his own accord.

"Good, saves me having to kill you," Tavistock thought and then despite herself fell asleep.

She woke a moment later because of the scream.

"What the ..." she mumbled, opening her eyes.

In front of her thick cigar smoke rose in grey pillars and beyond the smoke she could see the rapt and frightened faces of the audience arranged along the front seats of the dress circle. Those below her in the stalls were also watching the stage in rapt and horrified silence. All attention was fixed upon the hunched figure of a man. A grotesque parody, more ape-like than human. A man who had until a moment ago been the suave epitome of a tall, well-dressed gentleman.

"Well I wasn't expecting that," she said.

"Nor I, Sir," muttered Jack, who was sitting in the shadows of the curtained box.

Together they watched the *Strange Case of Dr Jekyll and Mr Hyde*. They saw how the hunched and demonic Mr Hyde beat a young woman to death, jumping on her mangled body and then with sickening callousness paid her grieving father to make it all go away. Jack was by then visibly shaken but Tavistock felt herself absolutely delighted.

"Well, what an actor, what a man," she breathed and then felt oddly and horribly excited. Sexually excited. The blood, the sound of the bones cracking underneath and the knowledge that no one would care. To go out into the dark and dismal depths of London society to prowl the mean streets, to hold that power of life and death, to be a plain Mister, that was power of a sort. Beside her Jack almost trembled in agitation.

"Scared, Jack?"

"Yes Sir."

"Why, it's only a play, a damn good actor and a lot of smoke and mirrors. A parlour trick, albeit a good one. Nothing to be scared about, nothing at all."

"No Sir." But Jack, who had watched the expressions of his young employer change as the play progressed, knew that nothing would ever be the same again.

A while later they left, mingling with the shocked and talkative crowd, a mix of the great and the good, the poor and the chattering middle classes. Deep within that crowd a woman who had been clinging to the arm of her beau, a cab driver from Shoreditch, stopped and stared, recognising the hurrying figure of one of the medical students she had helped several times on her ward.

Almost as if he sensed that he was being watched, the young man turned and stared back. The crowd closed in again and when the woman finally made it into the damp fog of a

London night he and his servant had gone, swallowed up in the murky, ill-lit shadows.

Jack and his master hailed a cab and while clambering in Jack could distinctly hear him humming a music hall tune. He grimaced; they had just watched one of the most disturbing pieces of theatre he had ever seen and his master was almost singing.

Tavistock was still singing as Richard shook her awake.

"Anyone here seen Kelly? Kelly from the Isle of Man."

Chapter 10

Richard and Tavistock sat in silence drinking their breakfast coffee as the news unfolded in front of them. Their eldest daughter Kate made a brief, happily grinning appearance in the doorway and after they had both wished her good luck, departed in a haze of perfume and hair products.

Richard put down his coffee mug and stared at his wife.

"Tavistock."

"Ummm."

"Tavistock, turn that idiot box off and listen to me."

Tavistock switched the television off with a flick of the remote and turned towards her husband.

"Look Tash, I know that when you are plotting a book you do all sorts of strange things." Tavistock raised an eyebrow but said nothing.

"However, this has got to stop."

"What has?"

"You keep going to sleep and when you do wake up, you wake up singing or you're waving that damn great knife around."

"What damn knife?"

"The one from the auction box, the one I caught you with last night."

"Last night?"

"Yes, last night. I found you in the kitchen with that knife, you were trying to hack a joint of lamb into bits."

"Oh come off it!"

"Well you were, and it has got to stop. Promise me – no more Jack the Ripper, no more music hall and no more wretched Victoriana."

"I promise," Tavistock airily replied. "If it means that much to you I will find somebody else to kill."

"Good, you could start with a civil servant or two," Richard advised her, getting up with a grin. "And now unlike our dear eldest daughter I will reluctantly go into the office."

Later Tavistock went upstairs to her study, and meaning to throw it into a box for storage in the depths of the garage, picked up the horn-handled knife.

Instantly she found herself in a dark, dank and dingy alley. Two figures stood in front of her and between them a woman was struggling. One of the men had one hand around the woman's waist and his other over her mouth, forcing her head back as his companion slashed her throat with what Tavistock realised was her hunting knife. The woman tried to kick out at her assailant but as the knife slashed again and the blood from her severed neck pumped out in a great spurt of bright red, she suddenly subsided, her eyes fading. She then slumped and slid down against the wall, her skirts riding up above her knees as she died.

"Jack, pull the trollop's skirts up," his companion hissed, his excitement in the kill still barely controlled.

Jack who had stood back from the woman as she expired stepped away and shook his head.

"Coward – I'll do it myself then." And with that the killer pulled the fabric up and slitting the bodice with his blade, exposed the woman's wrinkled and marbled naked flesh.

Swiftly he made the first incision, partly ripping open the abdomen.

"You see Jack, nothing to it. Who says I have to pay for my own cadavers, eh? This way I can save a fortune and still pass my anatomy exams."

Jack breathed out, almost ashamed of what he thought his young charge was about to do. "Now if I remember rightly the liver ..." He paused as the knife was thrust into the still warm flesh and a little blood oozed from the wound. There was someone coming towards them. In fact it wasn't just one and they sounded very drunk.

"Come on we'll have to leave this one. It's too damn public here, next time I'll do it off the street, and do it properly. Come on Jack." And so saying he picked up his discarded doctor's black bag and hastily shoved the knife inside.

"Come on," he reiterated, and adjusting his long coat, walked swiftly off into the night.

Tavistock stayed and tried to move towards the woman. But she was too late, time slipped around her and she was back, back in her own study and looking at the knife, the knife that had killed so many women, the knife belonging to the man universally known as Jack the Ripper.

Chapter 11

Kate Allan had, a few brief hours ago, been one of the happiest souls on Planet Earth. It was her first day as a fully qualified estate agent, after years of study and sheer hard work including the making of thousands of cups of indifferent tea and coffee. She had a cash buyer from London and four choice properties to show him: what could go wrong? As it happened, everything.

The plane from Gatwick had gone tech and arrived nearly two hours late, completely throwing her schedule and causing some terse conversations with her boss, the prospective buyer and an elderly seller who was in Kate's view a borderline nutcase. The first house had been a Georgian-style mansion recently built on the site of a two-bedroom bungalow. The prospective buyer, a Mr Ali, had taken one look at the immense front door, flanked by two pseudo-marble Doric columns and the few metres of carefully manicured lawn and marched back to the car.

The next house had been the complete opposite: a lurid pink pebble-dashed 1930s cottage surrounded by acres of land. Unfortunately most of the land around the house seemed to be under water and the front door was eight inches away from the TT course. Kate knew that it was eight inches because Mr

Ali had produced a ruler from an inside pocket and measured it. At that point Kate went back to her car and started the engine.

At the third house they visited they actually managed to get as far as the first floor and were about to view the panorama beyond the lounge window, when an elderly gentleman appeared in the doorway and advised them that he had called the police. Mr Ali was not amused at being called a come-over and it had taken some explaining and soothing of egos from both Kate and the lady from Meals on Wheels, who had turned up just as he was beginning to go puce, to stop him from suing the owner for making racist comments. Suitably mollified, he went back to the car and waited while Kate explained to her boss what had happened. It was at that point that the police arrived together with a social worker and the seller's irate daughter, who apologised profusely and tried to persuade Mr Ali to at least look around the house. Mr Ali smiled enigmatically from the passenger seat but refused to budge an inch, he just waited, arms folded until Kate got back in the car and then he demanded lunch.

During lunch Kate was informed by her colleague, Jill that the fourth house had that morning been taken off the market and so that just left Balla Fletcher, a dilapidated pile in the middle of nowhere, which was overpriced and allegedly haunted. Kate looked again at the details her boss had flung in her direction just as she was about to leave the agency that morning and her heart sank again before she reluctantly handed the brochure over to her companion, now in a slightly better mood due to an excellent Abbey Restaurant lunch.

"It has a piggery!" he exclaimed.

Kate nodded.

"And a well. I wonder if we will find pussy down it?"

Kate choked and gave him a sideways look. He looked

straight into her eyes and grinned.

"And yes, I do have a sense of humour."

She blushed a deep red and stalled the engine. Thankfully Mr Ali then immersed himself in the rest of the brochure and was still looking at the plan of fields and sundry outbuildings when they arrived at the house. Kate parked as close as she could get to the overgrown garden and after ensuring that Mr Ali had survived an attack by brambles and trailing fuschia attempted to undo the garden wire holding the latch and the gate together. Mr Ali waited patiently for a few minutes and then produced a pair of wire cutters from another pocket and with a deft movement cut the wire, kicked open the gate and proceeded to the front door.

The door hung drunkenly on one hinge and swung inwards with a metallic screech. A nasty smell of rot and damp vegetation greeted them and Kate sighed.

"Rising damp," she muttered.

"Really?"

"Yes, can't you smell it?"

"Oh yes but I rather think that it's been that high for years, don't you?" Mr Ali grinned at her and moved towards the stairs.

"Um …" Kate looked at him and then at the stairs, some of which had small, malevolent-looking fungi growing on them and announced that it might be better if they looked at the outside first. Mr Ali took one last look at the stairs and with a nod made his way back outside.

They walked in single file around the side of the building and as they did Kate stopped suddenly and turned to look back.

"What's the matter?" Mr Ali asked.

"I don't know … I just felt as if … oh, it's a bit silly really."

"That you were being watched?"

"Yes … how did you know?"

"Because I feel it too," Mr Ali explained as they both turned and faced the way that they had come. The old farmhouse looked blankly back at them. And Kate realised with a start that it was actually perfectly proportioned with its two floors of symmetrically placed windows around the central doorway. There was even a single round window in the attic, directly above the door and the large window below on the first floor. Along the roofline a dark and brooding row of Manx ravens watched them from unblinking coal-black eyes.

"Did you ever watch that Hitchcock film *The Birds* or are you too young?" Mr Ali asked, looking up.

"Yes." Kate replied. "Why?"

"That bit where they all sat along the telegraph wires and waited silently before attacking the children in the school yard?"

"Yes, we did it in Media Studies at school."

"Listen."

"What to? I can't hear anything."

"Exactly."

Mr Ali shrugged and then turning on his heel, set off towards the outbuildings. The piggery, a dark stone outcrop, emerged from the verdant and dripping leaves and as they approached it, Mr Ali stopped and sniffed the air.

"I thought you said that this place had been abandoned for years?"

"It has, the owners died about ten years ago leaving no immediate relatives and the courts have only just recognised the heirs."

"Hmmm."

"I mean, it took a firm of private detectives eight years to track them down and then another couple to sort out the estate."

"And who fixed the price?"

"My boss, when the market was high and everyone was knocking places like this down and rebuilding luxury mansions."

"And it still didn't sell?"

"No."

"Well it won't at the price it's on now … too much work and cost involved … I mean putting in the services alone would cost several thousands."

"And the rest."

"Exactly."

Mr Ali turned and smiled down at her, his blue eyes twinkling.

"And the real reason it hasn't sold?"

Kate shuffled uncomfortably and then decided to tell the truth.

"Because they say it's haunted, and not in a good way."

"And you can haunt in a good way?"

"Oh yes."

"I see."

Kate looked down at her feet and then further along the track. It was then that she spotted what her companion had already seen.

"Someone's already been here."

"You noticed."

"And …"

"Yes?"

"It sounds mad."

"Go on, after all you are talking to someone seriously considering making an offer on this magnificent ruin."

Kate laughed and then becoming serious again, looked more carefully around her.

"Well it looks like something was dragged through from

the wood and up to the piggery; I mean I presume that the building in front of us is the piggery."

"Yes I thought so too and also ..." He paused and wrinkled his nose in distate. "There is a smell."

Kate sniffed and then also caught the odour of something sweet, metallic and almost familiar.

"It smells like ..."

"A butchers?"

"Yes, one of the old-fashioned expensive sort with sawdust and ..." Kate's voice trailed off and she swallowed hard.

"You stay here young lady and I will investigate."

Kate stopped and watched until her companion faded from view as he dipped his head to enter the building. Seconds later he emerged very quickly and before she could move grabbed her arm and propelled her hastily towards the gate.

"You must ring your police force now," he urged, slowing to a halt as they reached her car.

"Now, without delay and then we will sit here and wait for them."

"But what do I say?"

"You tell them where we are and that we have found a body, which we suspect did not arrive under its own volition." Kate remembered the crushed grass and trailing weeds and then punched in the numbers 999 on her mobile phone.

Chapter 12

Detective Inspector Brian Clague stood in the doorway of the old piggery and took a deep breath. His hands shook and he momentarily and almost savagely craved a cigarette, something he had not done in years.

Behind him he could hear movement and eventually the thin, stooped form of the police doctor came and stood next to him.

"Well, I can certainly confirm that the poor bugger is dead, frankly don't think I've ever seen one that was deader."

"Nope."

"They should have the lights set up in a minute, as soon as they can connect the generator. Better for the photographs."

Brian nodded and went back to watching the surrounding woodland.

"How's young Kate?"

"Bit shaken, good thing she had that chap with her."

"Yes."

"Nasty, very nasty, haven't seen anything like …" He stopped mid-sentence and tried to remember something, something he had seen, something he had seen quite recently.

Brian, sensing his dismay, turned and watched as the clouds of memory parted and Dr Woods remembered in a burst of Technicolor.

"Mary Ann Nichols."

"Pardon?"

"You remember, Mary Ann Nicholls, 31st August 1888."

"Bit before my time, doc," Brian remarked drily.

"No you nitwit, Mary Ann Nicholls, the first of the Jack the Ripper victims."

"Jack the Ripper!" Brian glared at him as if he'd grown two heads, neither of which were attractive, and snorted, "Oh come on doc, this is 2012 and the Isle of Man."

"Well it might be, but unless I'm much mistaken he was killed lying on his back with two slashes to the throat, deep ones and then the lower part of his abdomen was ripped open by a long jagged wound. And don't forget the damage made to the genital area."

"Forget? I wish," Brian replied, frowning. "So which wound killed him?"

"Not sure, as yet. The pathologist will have a better idea when he can get him back to the lab. My guess is that he struggled and was then knocked unconscious before his throat was cut. Defensive wounds on the hands and arms and the blood spatter across the wall consistent with someone lying down and the arteries pumping up and out. Must have been fairly recent though as rigor hasn't entirely set in. Good thing young Kate and her companion have an alibi."

"They said they felt they were being watched," Brian mused, turning to stare at the blank back of the farmhouse. Darkened windows of broken glass and decaying lintels met his view, the lean-to porch leant drunkenly away from the wall, twisting skeins of deep green ivy clinging suffocatingly to its fragile frame.

Behind them the southern hills rose, wreathed in a descending grey mist which added to the feeling of claustrophobia emanating from the glen-locked house. Shadows fled across the waves of overblown grass and dock weed, as the sun retreated behind a band of blue-grey clouds.

"Funny thing really."

"What is?" Brian asked, a trifle peevishly.

"The Ripper angle."

"Why?"

"Our mutual friend Tavistock."

"Tavistock?"

"Yes, she's doing another book based on the Ripper murders, that's why I remember the name. I mean it was only a few days ago that we went through the old police files. You can get copies, you know."

"No I didn't," Brian mused before asking, "so Tavistock was working on what exactly?"

"The wounds – she wanted to know how deep they would have to be and if anyone could do it and I said …"

"You said what?"

"I said yes, anyone could."

They regarded each other coldly and then Brian stumped off towards the front of the house and the road.

When he finally reached the little knot of police and forensic staff he took a long deep breath and then marched towards two figures standing slightly apart from the rest. As he approached one of them ran towards him and without thinking he hugged the small slim frame before lifting her head and saying as gently as he could, "Kate, we need to ring your mum."

Chapter 13

Deep in the bowels of an old Victorian office block, a bent figure sat at an old-fashioned wooden desk and glared at a piece of paper he had just fished out of a wire tray marked 'Pending'.

"Barty!" he shouted.

A figure appeared from a hole in the floor and peered upwards myopically.

"What's this?"

Barty West hastened from the cellar steps and grabbed the offending paper which he attempted to read, very slowly and then handed back.

"It's a list, boss."

"How can it be a list? It only has one name on it."

"Not a list then," Barty agreed, hoping that would be that and he could get back to the filing and his game of three card brag with his internet gambling friends.

"Did you read the name?"

"Um … John Arthur … um … Callister."

"Yes, one of the banned and dark ones."

Barty slipped into a chair and regarded his superior with an interested stare; the cards could wait as he could almost smell an old and exciting story.

Mannanan Mac Lir erstwhile minor deity (third class failed) and guardian of the Isle of Man frowned at his employee with exasperation.

"What do you do down there?" he asked despairingly.

"Um … the filing," Barty replied, shifting uneasily in his seat.

"Well," Mannanan informed him in glacial tones, "if you had actually read the papers you are supposed to be sorting through you would know that this particular name is one to watch out for … especially as it's on a returns form."

"A returns form?"

"Yes Barty, a Callister has returned. A direct blood descendant of John Arthur."

"Right." Barty paused, no wiser. "And … er … what did he do this John Arthur Callister?"

"Do you remember the Ripper killings?"

"Yorkshire Ripper killed a load of prossies."

"I prefer the term ladies of negotiable affection."

"Sorry Boss."

"No not the Yorkshire Ripper, the London one, Jack the Ripper."

"Oh him."

"Yes him."

"My brother thought he was the cat's pyjamas, a real master, never getting caught or nothing."

"Your brother would."

They both sat thoughtfully pondering Barty's erstwhile brother, still languishing in one of Her Majesty's finest and securest establishments for amongst other things the murder of his brother Barty West, when a claxon sounded above their heads.

"What on earth was that?" Barty asked, looking upwards.

"Someone has returned to the Island and strangely enough

we have a murder on our hands."

"Oh good, field work," Barty grinned as he rubbed his hands in happy anticipation.

Mannanan looked again at the paper and frowned.

Barty, picking up a certain atmosphere, looked up and asked, "This John Arthur Callister, what did he have to do with Jack the Ripper … you don't mean … no he wasn't the actual Ripper … a Manxman was the Ripper? The bloody tourist board would do cartwheels …"

"No, *he* wasn't the Ripper," Mannanan informed him icily as he peeled his suit jacket from the back of his chair and shrugged himself into it. "John Arthur Callister was his assistant and … '"

"And what?"

"Never you mind what. Suffice it to say, that any relation of that man will not be looked on kindly by anyone, particularly me. It was bad enough the last time."

Barty looked up, his mouth falling open in the manner of a stunned fish, possibly a large red mullet, and stared at him.

"Barty."

"Yes Boss."

"Close your mouth, grab your coat and follow me, we have work to do."

And with that Mannanan promptly vanished, followed a moment later by his still grinning assistant.

Chapter 14

Tavistock Allan sat in her study and swung round and round on her swivel chair: it was no good, she would have to talk to someone about the thing now safely nestling at the bottom of an old cash box, which she had shoved into the bottom drawer of her desk and then locked. The key had then been thrown in the pond at the bottom of the garden. After which she had made a pot of peppermint tea which she had then taken with a packet of fig rolls, back up to her study.

Sighing heavily she got up, picked her way across and through the books perched and piled on every surface and peered through the grime-encrusted window. It was still raining and so she returned to her uncharacteristically tidy desk, her chair and her computer which still had a blank white square and the words Chapter 1 at the top.

She would just have to start again; maybe Richard was right and now was the time to kill off the current batch of health and safety, politically correct do-nothings who appeared to be running the civil service.

It was while she was tidying her envelope and pen drawer that she had the idea. It was blazingly simple and somewhere she had all her old research material. Suddenly galvanised, she began rooting through the old files and accumulated papers until she found the copies of all the original documents pertaining to the Jack the Ripper murders. An old story, a new twist and lots of blood and gore, perfect for a darkly comedic writer such as herself. All in all a good and productive morning even if she had only written two words.

"And I won't be breaking my promise to Richard at all as I'll be writing about the man that assisted Jack the Ripper and not Jack the Ripper himself, even if he was actually called Jack." She stopped and even managed a faint grin as she remembered some of her earlier dreams. Good to have at least one named character, especially as I have no bloody idea at all about who Jack the Ripper actually was. Except for the fact that I know he came from a good middle- or upper-class family and that he was a medical student and …"

She sat down again, the excitement beginning to leave her as the awful truth began to hit instead. "And he had Manx connections. In which case that bugger Mannanan probably knows all about it."

She was still running possibilities and methods of tackling Mannanan on the subject when the phone rang.

"If this is Emily wanting to come home rather than do Media Studies I will …" Tavistock briefly thought before barking "Yes" into it.

"Mum … ?" The words seemed strained and it was with difficulty that Tavistock recognised the muted tones of her eldest daughter Kate. Tavistock searched around in her brain and came up with the information that today was Kate's first day as a fully qualified estate agent and that she was showing some up-and-coming property tycoon an old house no one had yet managed to sell, despite a recent massive price drop.

"Kate, how did it go? Wasn't he interested?"

"Mum … I …" there was the sound of faint muttering and then a male voice came on the line.

"Tavistock, is that you?"

"Um yes, who is this … Brian?"

Tavistock was stunned: what on earth was Detective Inspector Brian Clague doing buying up dilapidated ruins?

"Why are you interested in that old dump?" Tavistock asked.

"I'm not."

"Oh? Then …"

"Can you get down here as quickly as you can; Kate's given her statement so she's free to go …"

"What statement? What do you mean *free to go* … ?" There was a brief hiatus and then her daughter was speaking again.

"Mum I found a body and I've been sick and … can you come and get me?"

"On my way."

Tavistock grabbed her car keys and her mobile and slammed out of the house. Behind her shadows deepened and a feeling of menace crept towards her across the recently mowed lawn.

Chapter 15

Fion Mandrake took another sip of champagne and settled down into the familiar heady perfumed bubbles and let her mind wander. In her head a checklist appeared and between sips she ticked off various lines one by one. The nanny had taken both children to their respective schools and had then gone into Douglas to purchase various items necessary for a two-week holiday in St Lucia. The housekeeper was awaiting the arrival of the caterers her best friend Elizabeth had recommended and the marquee was already up. Later she would have to talk to that rather dishy guy in charge of the jazz band; pity he was married but nobody was perfect. She paused and there and then decided not to wear her husband's favourite LBD but the rather striking red silk by Roberto Cavalli that she had purchased in London the previous week. She looked down at her new breasts and felt wonderfully young and sexy.

Somewhere in the distance a bell rang, she heard a door slam and then just as she was wondering whether to pour another glass a high-pitched scream of terror which was abruptly cut off.

Suddenly sober she half-slipped, half-hauled herself from the jacuzzi and completely nude apart from a few lingering swathes of foam raced to the bathroom door and locked and bolted it. Grabbing a towel from the floor, she covered most of her nakedness before crouching wide-eyed and trembling by the side of the door. She listened intently, every nerve straining to hear any sound, however slight. Minutes ticked slowly by until she could have sworn she heard something being dragged along the corridor outside. Almost directly opposite her bathroom door the noise stopped as if whatever was outside was listening for something inside. Fion shivered and tried to breathe into the towelling robe clutched about her. She hoped it would at least deaden the sound enough to make the listener think that there was no one there. The door handle twisted and she could feel the doorframe being pushed.

After what seemed like hours but was in fact merely seconds the dragging sound continued until it faded away.

Fion waited until she could hear nothing at all and then shivering from fear and cold slowly crawled, making as little sound as possible, to her mobile which she had casually left on top of her discarded clothes. Carefully she scrolled down the menu until she found the number of the company responsible for security and touched the call icon.

"Mr Callow."

"Yes, who is that, I can hardly hear you?"

"It's me. Fion Mandrake, Oliver's wife."

"Ah Mrs Mandrake, and what can I do for you?"

"Can you come now? There's someone in the house. I was in the bath and heard a scream and then this horrible dragging noise and now I can't hear anything at all and I'm so scared … and …"

"Where's Mr Mandrake?"

"I don't know, I mean he was in his study doing something on the computer but it wasn't a man's scream it was a woman's, and if it was a woman's why didn't he help?"

"Perhaps he went out?"

"No, he always tells me. Always … it's annoying."

"Right. Ah, got it."

"What?"

"The live feed from your house. Now that is odd."

"What?"

"It's not live any more but appears to be looped unless it really is 11.30a.m."

"That was when I decided to have a bath, or maybe a bit later."

"And you're still in there?"

"Yes, actually it's the family bathroom but it's the biggest and has a lock on the door."

"And it's now locked?"

"And bolted."

"Good, stay in there until I come and let you out. Clive my partner will test all the systems and I'll be there in about seven minutes with our latest employee primed and ready with one of the largest guard dogs you've ever seen"

"Thank you." Fion tried not to but suddenly found herself crying quietly into the phone.

"Don't you worry love; I'll be there almost as soon as you've got some clothes on."

"What?"

"Your new phone appears to have a very good camera, just thought you ought to know before you ring anyone else."

"Good God!"

"Not that I'm complaining, mind." Bob Callow chuckled as he reached the company van containing the aforementioned hound and his handler.

"Please hurry."

"On my way as you can hear from the fearsome and vile

engine noise. Now switch me off and wait three seconds because Clive will then be on line and can tell you exactly what's going on."

***

Bob arrived at the gated entrance to Mandrake Mansion House and stopped. The gates were half-open and the security camera which should have been glinting with an evil red eye from the top of a large carved lion clutching a ball wasn't, in fact it wasn't doing anything because it wasn't there.

"Clive," he muttered as he fumbled with the Bluetooth.

"What?" asked a disembodied voice with a distinctive Wirral accent.

"The gate is ajar and the camera is nowhere to be seen."

"Hang on … ah … Houston we may have a problem."

"Great!"

"It's still working but all I can see is a frond of something vegetable and a confused bunny."

"A bunny?"

"Yep." Ah, the gate should be fully opening now."

In front of him the gates swung inwards and Bob drove slowly and carefully down the drive. He stopped at the shrubs and plants at either side of the turning circle which faced the front door of an impressive modern Georgian-style mansion and switched the engine off.

"Anything going on in there?" he asked aloud.

"Nope, I've got all the feeds up and on real time. Someone certainly knows their way around a computer but not, luckily for us, as well as me."

"And?"

"Nothing, the whole house appears to be entirely bereft of life. Gardens clear and nothing nasty lurking in the outbuildings, according to the infrared and heat sensors."

"Right, I'll send the lad in. Pete – off you go and take the hound with you."

A large shape clothed from head to toe in a dark shade of grey detached itself from the back of the van together with one of the largest looking dogs Bob had ever seen. It was an ex-police dog fully trained and raring to go.

Together the young man and his companion merged into the bushes and headed off towards the side of the house.

Bob waited in the van and looked with interest at the small screen now displaying their careful progress.

"He's in," Clive advised.

"I can see that."

"Those new head cams are bloody good you know, excellent quality."

"Should be for the price," Bob sniffed.

"He's going through the kitchen – hang on, he's stopped."

"Bob," Pete muttered his voice lowered to almost a whisper.

"Yep, what you got?"

"Signs of a struggle. Looks like somebody was putting stuff away in the fridge and was grabbed from behind. Bits of canapé everywhere and a pool of something red and sticky under an overturned chair … nope ketchup or tomato sauce of some kind, hint of basil and garlic … Do not eat that! … Sorry, having disciplinary problems due to a large tray of upturned sausages … you do not like mustard and honey glaze … told you so … bet the daft bugger is sick again … Corridor clear … no one in the study, again signs of a struggle and the French windows into the garden are open … lounge clear, library clear … corridor empty … shit …"

"What?" Bob and Clive whispered in total unison.

"Blood, a big pool of blood at the bottom of the stairs

and then patches of it going up, looks like something was dragged upstairs and along the landing. Clive – anything on the screens?"

"Nothing, Pete lad. What's the dog doing?"

"Nothing – he's had a bit of a sniff and now he's just … right he's going up and I'm following."

"He's stopped outside a door second on the left and appears to be listening."

"According to the design plans that's the bathroom Mrs Mandrake should be in," Clive advised.

Pete paused and then after looking around again tapped gently on the bathroom door.

"Mrs Mandrake, it's me, Pete. I'm going to check the rest of the house and then I'm coming back and I'll escort you out."

"Oh Pete, thank God." They could hear a sob and then Pete moved on up the corridor, lined with beautifully painted cream doors, marred at intervals by smears of something dark and sticky.

At the end of the hallway, the dog stopped, whined and then sat and stared pointedly at a closed double door. Pete stood to the side of it and then with a sudden burst of speed hauled it open and crouched on the ground ready to cope with anything.

"Airing cupboard full of linen and something covered in a white sheet."

Bob and Clive watched as Pete carefully peeled back the heavy cotton to reveal the inert body of a middle-aged woman wearing a smart, plain black suit and no shoes.

Pete knelt down next to the body, sniffed and then straightened up.

"Chloroform at a guess from the smell and acid burns round the nose and mouth. She's still breathing though and I'll bag the rope just in case our assailant wasn't wearing gloves."

Pete busied himself with the woman's bonds and then left her turned on her side with a folded blanket under her head and another over her back.

The dog watched and then started to sniff at the last door along the passage.

"Be careful, Pete," Bob instructed, studying the camera feeds that Clive was still relaying.

Pete listened at the door and then flung it open and dived in, rolling to one side as he did so. There was no one there but the room itself was in chaos, bed linen had been flung around, furniture overturned and several cushions and one chaise longue had been ripped open with a knife of some kind. Photographs in silver frames had been smashed and along one wall a large smear of blood was still oozing gently towards the floor.

Pete moved carefully towards it, making the minimum of disturbance and gingerly touched the still sticky surface.

"That's odd," he murmured with a faintly puzzled frown.

"What is?" Bob asked

"It's still a bit runny and it shouldn't be, also ..." Pete looked around and then moved to the French doors leading onto a small wrought-iron balcony. The doors were half-open and banging against the doorframe as the wind eddied around that side of the house. There was a dark pool of red in the centre of the balcony between two large ornate planters embellished with fruit and stylised ivy. "There appears to be rather too much of it."

Bob stroked his chin thoughtfully and again regarded the scene. "Who would have thought that the old man would have had so much blood in him?"

Pete regarded the silent and staring dog now sniffing at the planters and rolled his eyes, the dog promptly sat and Bob was sure grinned at him.

"Okay I'm coming in, I'll have a word with Mrs Mandrake and then I'll do a search for Mr Mandrake, Clive's already got in touch with the police and the ambulance is on its way as I suspect that the lady in the cupboard is the housekeeper."

Pete and his canine companion took one last look at the room and careful not to step on the smeared blood, made their way towards the central staircase. Bob met them at the top and then they both moved towards the bathroom door.

"Mrs Mandrake, Fion, its me, Bob Callow, would you open the door please?"

There was a momentary silence and then they could hear a bolt being drawn back and the lock clicked. Slowly a youngish woman peeked out and then almost stumbled into the corridor. The dog, who had up to that point been avidly sniffing the skirting board, bounded towards her, got up on his hind legs and carefully placing both paws on her shoulders licked her nose and stared adoringly into her eyes. Fion staggered and then laughed out loud while crying at the same time. Salty tears were licked away and the dog woofed happily.

"Get down, Mr Pickles." Pete barked authoritatively. "Leave the poor woman alone, she's been through enough today without you trying to eat her."

"Mr Pickles?" Fion laughed as the dog released her and then sat at her feet panting with a large expanse of pink tongue lolling from his mouth. "Isn't that rather an er … odd name for a police dog?"

"Ex-police dog, did all the training but unfortunately failed his finals on the grounds that he's a pig."

"A pig?"

"Yep, the bold softie went haring after the suspect, pulled him to the ground and then after finding a bar of chocolate in his jacket pocket let said criminal go while he devoured half a pound of Cadburys finest."

"Ah."

"Can't really have a dog running around who would be more interested in the contents of the fridge than an armed raider and could be bribed by the mere smell of confectionery."

Pete fondly ruffled his dog's large silky ears and Mr Pickles sighed in ecstasy and collapsed in an untidy hairy heap at Pete's feet. "Mind you, he looks scary enough and he's very fast and very silent, also he's more bloody intelligent than most people," Pete added with a certain amount of pride.

Bob rolled his eyes and then had a sudden moment of inspiration.

"Mind if I have another look in the master bedroom?" he asked.

"No," Fion Mandrake asserted with a shrug, following him down the hallway.

When they reached her bedroom and saw the mess Fion took a deep breath before entering, her hands shaking with a combination of fear and anger.

"What the hell ..." she gasped, looking around her.

"Anything missing?" Bob asked, moving towards the open wardrobe doors.

"How could I possibly tell?"

"Well at a rough guess I'd say someone was looking for something and getting in a right strop when they didn't find it."

Fion shook her head and went to pick up a fallen perfume bottle. Bob gently stopped her and then took out his mobile and punched in a few numbers.

"No love, leave it for the police, they'll be here soon; I mean we might get lucky and get a print off something ... I mean they might get lucky ... ah Brian, I'd like to report a missing banker ... what? ... Er where?"

He had just opened a large wardrobe door which seemed to contain the entire contents of Peter Louis's menswear department when Brian asked "I don't suppose your missing client would have been wearing what looks like a handmade suit and very expensive polished shoes?"

"Um …" Bob stood in front of Oliver Mandrake's vast collection of designer clothes and sighed.

"Oh yes, I'd say he could very well be wearing something of that ilk."

Pete, who had at that point returned minus Mr Pickles, saw something in Bob's face and stopped in the doorway.

"Brian, I'll be there in about fifteen minutes, maybe ten."

Bob cut the connection and turned towards Pete while trying not to make eye contact with Fion Mandrake. "Um Pete, could you escort Mrs Mandrake out and wait for uniform to turn up as I have to meet with a member of the local constabulary?"

Bob Callow moved very quickly after that and after depositing Mr Pickles and the container of hot drinks and snacks on the drive, which Mr Pickles was told to guard, drove at speed towards the south of the Island and Brian's unidentified cadaver.

Chapter 16

From the dark and dingy doorway of a decaying cottage half hidden in gorse and brambles a black-coated shape peered through powerful German binoculars at the activity in the ancient farm below. Satisfied that all was in order, a small notepad was extracted from an inside pocket together with a thin gold pen. Carefully the pages were turned until a list of names appeared. Two had already been crossed out and as a swirl of mist curled its way downwards another name was neatly bisected with a sharp, blood-red line.

"Three down and four to go," the figure chuckled.

***

Kate clung to her mother and vividly reminded Tavistock of the day when Kate had decided that she didn't want to go to school and no one was going to make her; she was four and absolutely determined to be a limpet. Tavistock stroked her hair as she had done on the day of rebellion and whispered the soothing mantra passed down through the generations that everything would be all right, that mum would sort it out. Slowly the tightly gripping fingers unwound and with a shudder Kate let go and became a twenty-one year-old independent career woman.

Tavistock took a step back and then went over to Mr Ali who had been watching mother and daughter with a slightly twisted expression on his face. Kate followed her mother and swiftly introduced her client.

"Mum this is Mr Ali from London, Mr Ali this is my mother Tavistock Allan."

"Ah, the writer, I have read many of your books and the name is Ashleigh, Tobias Ashleigh and I have no idea where the confusion with it being Ali came from." He watched as Kate's face froze and then with a laugh added, "My secretary made the initial call and I'm afraid she had a very bad cold, so bad I sent her home if I remember rightly."

"I'm really and truly sorry," Kate apologised, red with embarrassment.

"Ah well, what's in a name anyway? Besides I rather liked being thought of as some sort of Moorish exotic, rather than a rather boring builder from Essex who had just holidayed in the Maldives for two weeks."

"Oh dear," Tavistock laughed.

"That old git this morning thought he was some sort of Arab terrorist," Kate muttered.

"Really?" Toby Ashleigh exclaimed. "Well that certainly accounts for his calling the police."

"It wasn't you," Kate hastily interrupted. "It was me, he apparently hates estate agents and is convinced it's all a con and I'm just casing the joint for an international gang of thieves."

"I see."

"According to his daughter he thought we were there to nick the silver." And with that Kate burst into almost hysterical laughter.

It was at that point that Bob Callow arrived to be greeted by an unsmiling Brian Clague and a departing team of forensic scientists clutching a variety of sealed plastic bags and what looked suspiciously like a large blue plastic cooler-box.

"Brian."

"Bob."

"So let's have a look at your cadaver then," Bob muttered almost cheerfully.

Brian gave him an odd look and then led him out and down a now flattened path to the well-lit piggery.

Bob stood and looked down at the remains of what had once been a middle-aged man and then left hastily to throw up in a bunch of nettles nursing the fern and moss-covered side wall.

Brian waited until his old mentor had regained his composure and then offered him an extra strong mint.

"Thanks," Bob muttered, sucking at the powdery tablet.

"Well – is it your banker?"

"Nope, thank God."

Brian sighed and looked again at the looming woodland. "Do you still employ the Hound of the Baskervilles?" Brian asked.

"Mr Pickles. Yes – why?"

"Best nose in the business, if I remember rightly."

"Oh yes that dog can smell sweeties a mile away."

"Good. Any chance you could get him and his handler here within say the next half hour or so?"

"Certainly, why?"

Brian took a mint and as he squirrelled the remainder of the pack away in a side pocket turned to face the old farmhouse now gently fading in the approaching twilight.

"Whoever did this didn't come from the house but from the wood and it would be interesting to discover if he came with the victim or if the victim met him here. The victim was wearing a rather pungent and expensive aftershave according to one of the boffins, who apparently has to buy bottles of the stuff for her brother-in-law every Christmas. The perpetrator would have been at some time covered in blood and would presumably have returned the way he came."

"Really? And you have deduced this how?"

"Old fellah across the road has been cutting a field for hay and says he saw a man go round the side of the house earlier on today before Kate and her client turned up. Thought nothing about it until we turned up as the place has been up for sale for ages. Lots of odd folk turn up, have a skeet around and then bugger off. He says he thought that maybe the first fellah had found the road through the woods and gone back that way."

"The road through the woods?"

"Yep – one of those mysterious hidden ones."

"Very hidden." Brian and Bob looked at the swaying shrubs, gorse, hawthorn and ash in front of them and failed to detect any sign of a pathway let alone a road.

"How did he get here?" Bob asked.

"The victim or the unsub?"

Bob sighed deeply. "Bloody American television has a lot to answer for. The victim. Look at it this way: Mr Nosey from across the way saw him come from the front of the house, so where is his vehicle? He can't have walked; this place is in the middle of nowhere, nearest house over a mile away and no bus route."

"Bike?"

"Then where is it?"

"We need Mr Pickles."

"Yes we most certainly do, and before it gets dark."

***

Mr Pickles arrived in the back of Pete's white van and wagging his tail, snuffled first at a handkerchief covered in Armani aftershave and then at the garden wall where he stopped and sat thoughtfully for a full thirty seconds before heading off down the road. Bob, Brian and Pete followed on behind until Mr Pickles came to the small stone bridge which spanned a shallow, brackish stream. Mr Pickles sniffed again and then proceeded over the bridge and up the twisting track until he came to a footpath which joined the road and then headed on up the hill.

Pete reached him first and after checking the wooden signpost, shrugged and told his four-legged partner to carry on. With a short happy woof, Mr Pickles jumped the stile, leapt over the small dry stone wall and hared up the grassy footpath and out of view.

Two minutes later as Brian struggled over the stile they all heard a series of frantic barks and then a long low growl which set the hairs on the backs of all their necks quivering.

"Shit," Pete muttered and raced away and up the hill.

Brian and Bob caught up with him at the top of the rise and watched as Mr Pickles pawed at something half-buried in a patch of damp gorse. Bob and Brian parted the encroaching brambles and revealed an old iron gate still barring the way to something on the other side of the gorse and hawthorn bushes surrounding it.

Mr Pickles then moved slowly around the vegetation, found a gap in a low stone wall, vaulted it and then barked loudly when he landed on the other side. All three men clambered as best they could over the wall and found to their astonishment that the land on the other side dropped dramatically away, and was in fact an old cart track which led directly to an old Manx cottage at the base of the bowl-shaped valley. Smoke curled lazily upwards from a side chimney and yellow light spilled out across the mown strip of grass in front. Mr Pickles, upon seeing that they had made it over the obstacle, bounded off down towards the path and stopped panting at the front door.

He then barked loudly until they caught him up and snuffled up and down the gravel path in front of the house until he found the scent again and with another woof ran off around the side of the house to a shiny grey and expensive top-of-the-range Land Rover parked under a makeshift carport of old wooden stakes and corrugated plastic.

Brian looked at the Land Rover and then at Mr Pickles.

"You clever dog," he asserted, removing his mobile phone from his jacket pocket. "Brian here, I need a check on a vehicle number, grey Land Rover, Mylchreest number plate MMN-732-N. Also I'm standing outside Myrtle Cottage, up the way from the crime scene, no idea how to get to it but there's smoke coming from inside and the lights are on ... Good, do that."

Brian broke the connection and then looked thoughtfully at the cottage, but as he did so he heard a vehicle being driven upwards, the gears grinding in disgust. Slowly another older Land Rover rumbled towards them up the hill and then stopped at their feet. A woman got out and glared at them, closely followed by two large dogs of various ancestry, mostly spaniel and possibly beagle. Her companions stopped dead when they saw Mr Pickles, who was now sitting bolt upright and quietly watching beside the other vehicle.

"You can't park that bloody thing there!" the woman barked, glaring at them. "It's private property."

"It's not our vehicle," Brian replied.

"Then who the hell's is it?" she asked.

"I have no idea," Brian replied before opening up his warrant card and introducing himself.

Chapter 17

Bob and Brian sat outside the Gluepot in Castletown and watched as an inept sailor attempted to battle the incoming tide and move his pristine and newly bought yacht out of the harbour. The local harbourmaster who was also watching sighed,scratched his head and ambled away to get a better view from the other side of the long narrow bridge over the harbour entrance.

"He'll never do it like that," Bob muttered.

"Yep, you're right as always. Ooh, but that's going to cost a bit," Brian agreed, taking a long pull on his pint.

"Mr Pickles get home okay?" Brian asked after a short companionable silence.

"Yep, at this very moment he is according to Pete tucking into fish, chips and a large spoonful of Branston Pickle while watching the opening ceremony."

"Branston!"

"Hence the name Mr Pickles."

"Wonder if Cav will get a medal?" Brian mused, squinting into the setting sun.

"Wonder if any of them will. My money's on young Kennaugh though."

"Hmmm ... speaking of money, found out who the Land

Rover belonged to."

"Really?"

"Some investment banker called Nyles Wilson, works as a freelance money man, bit dodgy according to the FSC who are currently turning their beady eyes on one of his old partners."

"Oh?"

"A rather shady individual who just happens to be your missing banker."

"Well I hope they don't find anything until he pays his last bill," Bob muttered, opening up a pack of pork scratchings.

"How can you eat those things?" Brian asked with a shudder.

"Easy, watch."

"You do realise that someone is killing off bankers?"

"Couldn't happen to a nicer bunch," Bob observed, watching as the yacht foundered and hit a small fishing boat moored on the other side of the harbour. Several young men launched themselves from the side entrance of the pub and started shouting loud and anatomical threats to the hapless yachtsman, before swaying purposely towards the bridge.

"Hope he sorts himself out before they do," Brian observed darkly.

"Won't matter, you're off duty," Bob advised, chewing on a scratching.

"As if that will make any difference," Brian retorted.

"True, very true."

They watched amiably as the yacht was finally turned at almost the same time as the tide and with seconds to spare and with the engine working at maximum the thing shot out of the harbour like a cork from a bottle.

"Hope he doesn't come back for a bit," Bob asserted as he took another gulp.

"Not likely to, managed to get a berth in Peel Marina," Brian stated authoritatively.

"And you would know this how?"

"Ah – I also have my sources oh mighty and venerable one."

"Less of the venerable you cheeky sod."

"Another?" Brian asked, picking up his empty glass.

"Might as well. Moira said she would drive me home after Weight Watchers, so I have …" Bob peered at his watch, "at least an hour to go allowing for the usual chat time."

After a while Brian returned and after dumping another amber-coloured pint in front of Bob, tentatively broached the subject which had been uppermost in his mind.

"How well do you know Tavistock?" he asked.

"Tavistock … well for ever I guess – we met in Reception only then it was known as the Infants and went up through the ranks, until that is, she left for that posh girls' school across, why?"

"You don't think that she would do anything a bit, well, nuts … purely in the interests of science and er … literary research?"

"Like putting belladonna in the horseradish sauce to see who will throw up first, that sort of thing?"

"Yes, that sort of thing."

"No."

"Right."

"Why? And Brian as you have just maligned one of my oldest and best friends the explanation had better be bloody good."

"It's this Ripper thing."

"What Ripper thing?"

"I was talking to old Doc Woods and …"

"What, old Bernard's still around?" Bob asked in surprise.

"Yes. And he said that …"

"Surprised he's not in a box himself by now …"

"Bob, will you just shut up for a brief moment or two?"

"Sorry lad, you were saying –"

Brian took a deep breath and glared at his companion. "What I was trying to say was that Tavistock is doing a book on Jack the Ripper and …"

"Brian lad, hundreds of writers have done stories about that mad bugger, even that writer what's her face … Scarpetta? Scarletta?"

"Patricia Cornwall."

"That's the bunny. Anyway, it's just a story and …"

"She was asking Doc Woods how hard you would have to hold a knife to make the wounds in the neck like he did and if you needed special knowledge and he said no."

"And your point is?"

"She was asking yesterday, the day before we find the body. The day before her daughter was showing someone round the crime scene. And the odd thing is that if the plane from Gatwick hadn't have been delayed Kate would have been showing that Ashleigh chap round before the murder was committed."

"Oh."

"Yes, oh."

"Tavistock knew Kate was showing him the house because she wanted to know why I wanted to buy a dilapidated old ruin. And Kate only knew about showing him around that morning."

"Look Brian, I can see where you might be going with this but why would Tavistock want to kill someone? I mean she does it all the time in her head."

"Which is kinda my point," Brian agreed softly.

Bob looked at him over the rim of his glass and slowly

and carefully set the pint down on the wooden table between them.

"You can't be serious?" Bob asked incredulously.

"I'm not, but you have to admit it doesn't look good and she has absolutely no alibi for the time in question."

"Which is?"

"Around twelvish"

"About the same time as my banker went missing."

"Is it?"

"Yes, and you know something? I have a strong hunch that he has more to do with this than Tavistock writing a book on some Victorian serial killer, and I'd lay odds on the fact that my absconding banker knew your cadaver."

Brian sat back and regarded his old mentor and friend in a thoughtful fashion.

"In which case do we have one body or two?"

"Your guess, Brian old pal, is as good as mine."

Chapter 18

Clara stirred the glowing embers of the fire with a long thin poker and watched as sparks flew outwards and then danced and jigged up the soot-begrimed chimney. Her two dogs lay twitching and drooling on the hearthrug in front of the Victorian fire grate and chased imaginary rabbits as they dreamt long, warm, doggy dreams.

Careful not to disturb them, she threw another log onto the fire and settled back into her chair. It was an old, dull-red leather wing chair she had bought at auction and was far more comfortable than many a designer sofa she had bought when she still had the large manorial pile and the income to match.

Outside her cottage the fog drifted past her lounge window in long strands of opaque white, silently catching on bedraggled hedgerows of gorse and fuschia heavy with tubular bells of deep claret edged with dark purple anthers and stamen.

Clara wondered about putting the television on and watching the start of the London Olympics but couldn't be bothered. In fact lately she couldn't really be bothered about anything. She knew she ought to at least eat and so grudgingly levered herself out of her chair and walked around the chimney breast and into the kitchen at the back. On the other side of the lounge, directly opposite the front door a steep staircase gave access to the one bedroom in the eaves. Behind the staircase and next to the kitchen lurked a tiny bathroom.

Clara looked around her and felt oddly content. It was small, it was tidy and it was entirely hers. No bank could foreclose on it and no administrator seize it.

She opened the fridge and was still standing undecided when there could clearly be heard a soft but insistent tap on the front door.

"Go away," she muttered as she withdrew a box of eggs and a tub of low-fat spread from the fridge. Bread was extracted from the breadbin and fed into an electric toaster and the already partially filled kettle was switched on. The tapping stopped and then started again but this time directly in front of her and on the back door.

Clara stopped and looked in horror as the door knob moved from side to side.

"But that's impossible," she gasped. Only the day before she had tried to cut down some of the overgrown weeds and clear a path to the back but had given up when she had realised that it was just too thick and overgrown, there also appeared to be part of a wall and a mound of rubble blocking the path around the cottage and she would need a small JCB to clear it properly.

The door knob stopped moving and then the tapping started again on the front door.

Clara, white-faced, stalked into the lounge, picked up the poker and carefully unlocked and unbolted the front door and peered out. There was absolutely no one there.

She stepped out into the soft velvety darkness and listened. A ewe could be heard calling to her lamb and all around water dripped from leaf to sodden leaf. A dog barked in the distance and somewhere further down the valley a car started and then rumbled away into the twilight gloom until it failed to register at all.

She looked up the track to the far-off hills and then down towards the valley and glen below and still failed to see any sign of life, human or otherwise. Thoroughly unnerved, she hastily retreated into the safety of her tiny home and swiftly relocked and bolted the white painted door. It was as she turned back towards the fire and the kitchen beyond that she saw the smartly dressed middle-aged man in a pinstripe suit sitting in the other wing chair opposite her own.

"What in God's name …" Her voice tailed off as a diminutive and rather rotund individual appeared in the doorway to the kitchen with one of her best porcelain cups in his hand.

"What on earth?" Clara exclaimed as both gentlemen looked towards her, her two dogs however remained completely oblivious to both intruders and slept stoically on.

"Ah Clara. Please do sit down," the gentleman in the chair advised, pointing to her recently vacated seat.

"But –" Clara found herself sitting and then waiting patiently for the invaders to say something else, anything else which would have broken the eerie silence now pervading her home.

Outside, beyond her front windows she could see the mountain mist thicken to a thick grey blanket of fog, which gradually obliterated every recognisable part of her normal view of track, rock, hedge, shrub and distant hill.

"You are Clara Callister aren't you?" the gentleman asked.

"Yes."

"And your great, great, great grandfather was John Arthur Callister?"

Clara started and managed to utter the words "Yes he was."

"Let me introduce myself. I am Mannanan Mac Lir and …

Ah Barty, many thanks."

The round gentleman had reappeared with a tray of tea things and after depositing it carefully on a low coffee table stood waiting patiently for further instructions.

"Barty, you may take the evening off," Mannanan advised.

"Yes Boss," Barty muttered, clearly none too pleased at being dismissed so soon.

"Now, Barty."

"Oh all right then." And before Clara's astonished gaze he completely disappeared with a faint popping noise.

"Milk, sugar?" Mannanan asked, raising the teapot.

"But …" Clara stammered, pointing to where the very solid form of Barty West had been standing up to a moment before.

"Poor Barty, he's a lousy assistant but he does make remarkably good tea," Mannanan informed her as he passed over a cup and saucer.

"What on earth … I mean who … I mean …"

"I like what you've done with this place by the way," Mannanan murmured thoughtfully as he picked up his own cup and saucer and looked around. "Your grandfather wasn't exactly a homebody."

"How?"

"Do I know this?" Clara nodded at him and took a tentative sip; it was actually really good, something she had not really expected and it was also real tea.

"I knew your grandfather. And yes I know it was a long time ago and people don't live that long but then I'm not exactly human."

"You can't possibly be Mannanan Mac Lir, because he's a god or a ghost or something," Clara blurted out.

"Well I'm not a god or even a minor deity any more but I

am still the guardian of this Isle and as such I have to ask you whether you are going to keep up the family tradition."

"The family tradition?"

"Yes."

"And this would be what exactly?"

"Let's not waste time, shall we young lady? The diary is upstairs in an old tin box together with an old cut-throat razor, which Barty informs me is still amazingly sharp and polished."

"It was a long time ago," Clara informed him with a smile.

"But old habits die hard."

"I have no intention of killing any prostitutes, male or female," Clara shouted at him.

"He assisted in that, I admit. Except for the last one."

"He had no choice. If you've read the diary you know that. He had no choice at all."

"On that point you and I are agreed. Unfortunately your late ancestor didn't just stop there."

"Oh?"

"Yes, oh. Which is why I asked him to leave the last time he set foot on my Island and he agreed never to return; he also more importantly promised me that he would destroy his weapon of choice. Something that he very obviously lied about."

"He gave it to my grandmother's mother's …"

"Spare me the genealogy, Clara."

"What do you want?"

"I want you to tell me why you have brought it back."

"It's a long story."

"Well in that case you had better throw another log on the fire, prepare that plate of eggs you were clearly thinking of eating before I turned up and between mouthfuls tell me the truth, the whole truth and nothing but the truth."

Clara nodded and did exactly as she was told. Later after she had sat and talked and talked she carried the tin box from its hiding place to the little coffee table and carefully unfolded the cloth in which the gleaming weapon nestled.

Mannanan sighed deeply and looked from her to the razor and back again.

"I see," he said and then sat back in his chair, steepled his fingers and stared long and hard into the steady flames of the recently banked fire.

"Just the once?" he finally asked.

"Yes, just once."

"And no more."

"No."

"Then you have my agreement on one condition."

"Name it."

"No blood must be spilled on this land."

"Agreed."

Mannanan raised himself from his chair and they solemnly shook hands, after which Mannanan disappeared, leaving the room as suddenly and as quietly as he had come.

Outside the fog thinned and blew away in fat bales of grey. Rolling and tumbling down the track towards the valley below. As it thinned the stars above the cottage twinkled into view one by one as a large blue-white moon crept slowly above the distant hills, sending rays of harsh white light downwards, lighting up the grassy knolls and twisted trunks of hawthorn, ash and willow.

Chapter 19

Tavistock Allan sat on the low stone wall and gave a long happy lick to the Davidsons Whippy ice cream she held in her right hand. In front of her a blues band played loudly from a long white gazebo and she happily joined in the festival feel by tapping out the rhythm with her feet. Richard had sauntered off after lunch at the Harbour Lights to watch the boats bobbing about in the bay and so Tavistock was enjoying five minutes peace and quiet and people-watching; after all, she told herself, you never know who you might see or what and it could all go down in a book.

She turned to watch a stilt walker flirting with a couple of barely clad teenage girls and caught sight of a Viking in full regalia buying dinky donuts from a van. She chuckled and took another bite of vanilla-flavoured heaven.

Richard had initially baulked at staying to see the floats after lunch in Peel but after listening to a very good steel band which had set up camp next to the restaurant and conveniently in front of the adjoining pub, had been quite happy to potter about after their Sunday lunch.

Children sauntered past clutching various items including quite a few plastic swords and oddly shaped helium balloons. A long dragon sashayed past, its paper-mache head and middle keeping time to the music while the denim-clad legs at the end desperately scuttled to keep up. Various motorised buggies trundled past bearing their elderly owners to the designated area in front of the swing bridge.

Tavistock closed her eyes briefly and for a fleeting moment was transported back to the athletics stadium where only the night before she and her sister had shouted themselves hoarse cheering on a selection of British athletes. She could still feel the euphoria as wave after wave of sound battered their senses. Three golds and she had been there, the perfect end to a very odd day. She was still reliving the moment when she felt a spot of rain and looked up, hoping that the weather would at least hold out until the floats had gone past. As she lowered her eyes from the scudding clouds she noticed a vaguely familiar face. For a moment the memory of who it belonged to failed to be retrieved from the internal filing room of her brain. The woman in question bent to untangle her two gundogs and as she straightened up she tucked a stray strand of greying hair behind her ears and simultaneously pushed her sunglasses back towards her eyebrows. It was then that Tavistock remembered and without bothering to think she shouted out. "Clara Callister, it can't possibly be you!"

Clara started and then turned towards the woman shouting out her name. For a brief moment she looked at Tavistock with a completely blank expression and then her face broke into a wide grin.

"Tavistock, as I live and breathe, how the hell are you?" Clara hurried over to her old friend and gave her a brief and loving hug.

"Well I never, budge up old girl and we can have a brief chat before the festivities begin." Clara settled down next to Tavistock to the growing amusement of the young couple who had been sitting on the edge of Tavistock's old beige cardigan.

"You know I've been trying to get hold of you but I couldn't remember your married name or where you lived," Clara informed her, as she tried again to untangle her dogs' leads. Both dogs sat panting at her feet and began to eye her friend's remaining ice cream with envious looks.

"I thought you had moved across, married some millionaire manufacturing giant," Tavistock observed, licking up the last of the ice cream and then carefully eating the wafer cornet. As the last crumb was eaten both dogs sighed and then settled down to sleep on the kerb below their mistress's swinging feet.

"I did but he died so I came back."

"Where are you living now then?"

"My grandmother's old cottage."

"Good grief, that tiny place up in the hills?"

"Yes."

"Oh."

"Actually it rather suits me, easy to keep clean, cheap to maintain now I've done the basics and the dogs love it."

"Right."

"So did you marry that chap you were so fond of? Bob something …"

"Bob Callow?" Tavistock laughed outright. "No, I married Richard."

"Somebody talking about me?" a deep voice asked in amusement. They both turned towards the speaker and Clara stood and held out her hand.

"Clara Callister, old schoolfriend of your wife."

"Richard Allan, husband of same."

"Good to meet you both. Look Tavistock, it's been great meeting again. Be good to catch up. How about coffee or lunch or something? I hear that new place The Abbey in Ballasalla is really good."

"It is and we must. Look, here's my card, it's got my email and telephone numbers on it. I'm free most of next week apart from Thursday when I'm doing a reading at the library but other than that it's the same old routine. Just give me a bell and we can meet up."

Clara took the proffered card and with a smile tucked it into her back pocket, and then she gathered up the leads of her reluctant pets and walked off just as the first part of the parade rounded the corner of the coastguard's building.

"Who was that?" Richard asked, taking up Clara's vacated seat.

"Old schoolfriend, haven't seen her in years. Odd though."

"What."

"Her coming back to the Island."

"Why? People do."

"I know, but Clara was different."

Richard turned and watched his wife as she strained to remember what it was that was bugging her.

"Anyway it will be nice for you to catch up. Get you out of the house."

"I was out of it yesterday and the day before."

"Not the same thing at all, it was mostly work."

"Got to go to the Olympics though."

"Yes, and I have no idea how Gerard managed to get hold of four tickets at short notice like that."

"Well according to my little sister by spending the last two weeks swearing at his computer."

"Speaking of which, Clive rang … you know Bob's nerdy partner … said he needed to talk to you about Mary Jane Kelly."

"Really, he's found something?" Tavistock exclaimed with

a squeak of delight.

"Apparently so, and he reckons you owe him at least one whole bottle of Scotland's finest."

"Great."

"Sometimes I really worry about you, Tash."

"I know and it really is very irritating. Oh look Richard, isn't that little kid too cute for words. Reminds me of George at the same age, only cleaner."

Tavistock smiled sunnily into her husband's eyes and then squeezed his hand as the tiny fireman waving a plastic axe strutted past them, closely followed by another float from which sweets were being thrown in wild abandon.

***

Some way away on the hill opposite the new marina a dark figure watched them both through a pair of binoculars. He wasn't at all happy that the two women had met and more worryingly he had no idea if it had been by accident or design. Either way it meant that things would have to be speeded up a pace. Carefully he returned the binoculars to their case and then extracted the small notepad from a zipped pocket. There were now only three names left on the list which hadn't been crossed through. Two would be very difficult to organise but the third would be a piece of cake in comparison. In fact so easy would it be that he was almost tempted to take a day or two off.

***

Tavistock woke suddenly, so suddenly that the dream she had been having fled, leaving a nebulous memory that something very important had just escaped her grasp.

Beside her Richard sat up and adjusting the pillows behind

his head, demanded to know why she had been singing and why that song, again?

Tavistock emerged from the cocoon of crumpled bedclothes and regarded him with bleary unfocused eyes as her brain tried to keep up.

"I don't sing," she muttered.

"You got that one right," her husband smirked from his side of the bed.

"And what, pray, was I singing?" she asked, fumbling for the glass of water on her bedside table.

"'Has anyone here seen Kelly?'" Richard replied, yawning.

"What!"

"Yep, the entire chorus and a couple of very rude verses I've never heard before and then you hit me."

"I didn't!" Tavistock squawked.

"You did, and then you lit an imaginary cigar and winked at me in a very lewd manner."

"You're making it up!"

"Am not."

"You must be, I mean I don't know the song for a start and why would I be smoking a cigar?"

"Search me. Coffee?"

Tavistock nodded and snuggled back under the duvet. What had she been dreaming of? Why that song? After all she had hidden the knife so there was nothing to take her back to that time or place – and why oh why did it seem so important?

It wasn't until the caffeine had taken hold and she was searching for clean underwear that it hit her.

Mary Jane Kelly – the last victim of Jack the Ripper.

Kelly from the Isle of Man.

Chapter 20

"Did you remember to get the milk on your way home like I asked you to?" Tavistock demanded of her yawning spouse as she attempted to cut herself a slice of bread.

"Uh, um, no – but it's okay," Richard mumbled through a mouthful of toast. "I like black coffee for breakfast."

"Well I don't!" Tavistock growled, clutching the bread knife. "And Emily has cereal."

Richard gave her a blank look and went back to the book he was reading.

Incensed, Tavistock thrust the bread knife into the bread board and stormed off to get dressed. Richard looked up to see the knife gently twanging from side to side and looked across to the cat who was sprawled in front of the radiator and half-heartedly cleaning one ragged ear with a none-too-clean paw.

"What was all that about?" he muttered. The cat stared at him as if he was an idiot too stupid not to know already and went back to sleep. Richard sighed and poured himself another coffee and then promptly forgot all about it until Brian Clague rang him at work later that morning.

"So, Richard," Brian declared in a jovial fashion, not sure how to broach the question uppermost in his mind.

"Brian."

"Have you got a minute?"

"For one of my favourite coppers, why not?" Richard sat back in his chair and straightened his back, the report in front of him gratefully ignored, as it had been written by a senior civil servant and was as understandable as an instruction manual for a nest of tables written in Mandarin.

"Ummm this is going to sound a bit ... well ... er ... strange."

"I'm married to a writer so I doubt if you even know what strange is, and she has friends," he added gloomily as an afterthought, "friends that make her appear almost normal in comparison. Please note the emphasis on the word normal."

"Well actually it's about Tavistock that I'm calling."

"Oh?" Richard replied, the first vestiges of unease creeping up his spine and making the hairs on the back of his neck begin to feel uncomfortable.

"Tavistock and her current obsession."

"Not Jack the bloody Ripper again!" Richard wailed.

Surprised by this, Brian could only reply, "Yes."

"I've told the stupid woman to stop. It's unhealthy and as for that bloody knife she found in London, it can ruddy well go back to the auction rooms it came from."

"What the hell are you talking about?" Brian asked.

"What am *I* talking about? What are *you* talking about?"

"I'm talking about the fact that Tavistock has been asking our police surgeon about exactly how hard you would have to slash at a neck to sever it and other questions of a macabre and forensic nature and by a horrible coincidence we have a body found by your daughter which has had its neck severed in exactly the same fashion as Jack the Ripper's first universally recognised victim and his abdomen was hacked open by exactly the same sort of weapon which forensics now agree could have been used by the original Ripper." Brian took a deep breath and then a restorative sip from his Costa Coffee cup.

Richard sat in his chair feeling stunned and gradually began to feel the world around him collapsing into a small charred heap. And he had the nasty feeling that it was he and he alone that had been holding the box of matches at the time.

There was a silence and then Brian cleared his throat and Richard who had hoped that up to that point Brian hadn't really been listening discovered that the habits of a lifetime had been changed and that he had.

"Tavistock has a knife?"

"Um yes."

"And she bought it at an auction in London?"

"Yes."

"And just how long has she had this knife?"

"Um – a week or so."

"And where is it now?"

"I have no idea. You see we had a bit of a row about it and she promised to get rid of it."

"Today?"

"Yes."

"She got rid of the knife today, the day after we have someone murdered, someone murdered in the style of the Ripper, with a knife you are convinced that your wife might have had in her possession at the time of the murder."

"Yes."

"Shit."

"My thoughts exactly."

"You do know that I'm now going to have to interview her?"

"Now look here Brian," Richard spluttered, "it was Kate that found that wretched man, Kate and her client. I mean even Tavistock wouldn't involve her own children. Oh God that came out all wrong what I meant to say was …"

"I know, I know. Unfortunately your daughter's client's plane was delayed getting into the Island yesterday and if it had been on time your daughter wouldn't have been anywhere near the place and as it was also a momentary decision by her boss that very morning to throw in the murder site Tavistock wouldn't have actually known that she would be going there. I mean you do see how it looks."

"Oh yes, I see all right."

"Oh and Richard," Brian hissed down the phone, "before you even think of warning her, I should tell you that I am standing on your front doorstep, I'm ringing the bell, and your wife has just opened it. Have a nice day."

And with that Brian disconnected before Richard could say or think of anything that would further incriminate his wife. Richard sat completely still for a moment or two which felt like hours but may have been minutes or possibly it may have been the other way round only by then he was too upset to really notice. At last he pulled himself together and hurriedly punched in Bob Callow's number.

"Bob!" he shrieked as Bob answered his mobile.

"Ah, Richard."

"Bob, that ex-colleague of yours, that viper in the bosom."

"Brian?"

"Yes Brian, he's gone stark-staring mad."

"Please tell me that he hasn't arrested Tavistock."

"Arrested!" Richard squeaked in an appalled voice. "He said he was just going to interview her."

"Right, well that's a bit better, last night he was all for arresting her."

"Shit."

"I told him it was a bad idea."

"Good, pity he didn't take any notice."

"You know they actually arrested and interviewed the actor portraying Dr Jekyll and Mr Hyde over the original killings?"

"Really, why?" Richard asked as he was mentally sidestepped.

"Someone reported him, a well-meaning member of the public who couldn't believe that any actor could possibly be that good."

"And you are telling me this why exactly?"

"Because Tavistock has a long list of writer friends and associates who have at one time or another been dragged into the local clink simply because they knew more than the police about some crime or other." Bob paused and then added. "Which in some cases wouldn't be difficult."

"And you were told this by?"

"Tavistock of course, she used to joke about it."

"Bob, it may not be all that funny now especially as I … er … I …"

"Spit it out Richard, it can't be that bad."

"I told Brian that Tavistock had promised to get rid of the knife."

"What knife?" Bob exploded.

"The knife she bought at auction, the one that she's now convinced belonged to Jack the Ripper himself."

"Bloody hell." Bob stopped in his perambulations around his office furniture and began to think. "Well, it will be easy to prove that it wasn't the murder weapon. All she has to do is give it to the police and they can have it forensically tested."

"That's just it. I rang her earlier 'cos I'd been a bit off with her before I left this morning and she told me she had got rid of it and no one would ever find it."

"She did what!"

"It was only what I'd asked her to do. She's been really odd since she got the wretched thing."

"Odd? Tavistock? Surely not," Bob muttered sarcastically.

"Yes odd, well odder than usual certainly. She's been having bad dreams, she goes to sleep all the time or blacks out, either way she can't remember what she's done and she sings in her sleep, this morning she made threatening gestures with a bread knife and all I'd done was forget the bloody milk."

"Tavistock."

"Tavistock." Richard sighed pensively as he remembered the impaled cutlery. "Bob, you don't think that there is any well ... possibility that she may be possessed. I mean she wouldn't actually ..."

"No, no I don't. Look, I'm going to ask around – in fact I may even go into my old office and make sure that everyone knows how nosey and interested I am. In the meantime get her a good advocate, that is if she actually needs one, and go home. We have to find that wretched knife and prove that she didn't use it."

Bob disconnected and after a moment's hesitation Richard grabbed the suit jacket from the back of his chair and with a brief shout of, "I've got to go – family emergency!" to his assistant, rushed out of the office, his car keys already clenched between his fingers.

Chapter 21

Tavistock arrived back home and went straight to her study. She was still fuming. Brian had arrived, hotly pursued by her husband, both of them had shouted first at each other and then at her and finally she had given up, gone and found a long-handled screwdriver and managed to open the drawer in which the knife had been hastily hidden.

"So much for bloody ponds," she thought, ruefully surveying the damage afresh.

The knife had been deposited into a plastic evidence bag and Brian had then departed, looking slightly mollified as the knife had very obviously not been recently used.

Richard had also then departed muttering various imprecations against the police, the Chief Constable and idiot wives in general. In fact so cross was he that he had actually sworn more than once, something he was not known to do. He had also informed her that he was going to be working late, as he had a lot of stuff to finish off.

Tavistock, incensed by the unfairness of it all, went shopping.

Now she was back and the initial anger had worn off to be replaced by a vague feeling of unease and a small helping of paranoia.

It was as she was sitting at her computer looking at a blank screen that the telephone rang.

"Yes," she barked.

"Is that the author Tavistock Allan?"

"Speaking."

"Oh Good, we got you. Look, I hope you don't mind but your publisher let us have your number and well someone has let us down and we were hoping that if possible you could come and do a reading and signing for us?"

"And you are?"

"Daunts Bookshop, in London. Our owner has a bit of an interest so to speak in the Island, his father having been at one time the Governor."

"Oh that Daunt, nice man," Tavistock murmured, warming to the caller.

"Yes, well the thing is, we'd like you to come tomorrow if that's at all possible. I mean I know it's short notice and all that. But could you be here by say lunchtime? Well a bit before actually. We'll pay for the flights to City airport and pay for a taxi from the airport … um is it ok if we reimburse you when you get here?"

Tavistock frowned; it was certainly unusual and normally she wouldn't leave the house unless the tickets, travel and where necessary hotel had already been booked and paid for but …

"I suppose I could do it just this once. Um, let me ring you back."

She put down the phone and then using 1471 rang back.

"Daunts Bookshop," said a voice.

"Hello, it's Tavistock Allan, I was just speaking to someone about a signing."

"Oh yes, that was me, actually could you hold for just one second … look it's over there under the history section, well yes it may be fiction to you but she's a historical novelist so … sorry about that, can you come?"

"Oh yes, and you are sure that I can be reimbursed?

"Of course, it's just that it's all last minute and I'm only the assistant manager and don't have the authority to book the tickets but the manager is back tomorrow and asked me to please get someone and as your my mum's favourite author I thought …"

"Right, fine, I'll book the tickets. I could do with a bit of a break," Tavistock added with feeling as she surveyed her ruined desk and remembered the looks on the faces of both her husband and Brian Clague as they stood and mutually scowled as she explained about locking the knife in the drawer and throwing the key into the pond.

"Um … are you working on anything at the moment?" the voice at the end of the line enquired, breaking her train of thought which had been growing ever more resentful.

"Well, I was thinking about a book based on the Ripper murders."

"Really? What fun. And very apt if I may say so."

"Oh why?"

"Because of the date."

"Date?"

"Yes, well, it's the 8th of September tomorrow."

"Oh?"

"The day Annie Chapman was murdered."

"Oh God yes." Tavistock paused a moment. "You seem very knowledgeable about the subject."

"I guess it's living so close to the original crime scenes and you wouldn't believe the number of titles we have in stock about it, and what with that new detective series on the Beeb early next year and the new Patsy Cornwall due out, well …"

"Yes of course, the Cornwall." Tavistock tried to keep the

bitterness out of her voice but realised she had failed miserably as the voice continued in a less effusive manner.

"Right … well … I'll sort out the posters and let the local press know that it's to be a different writer. I've already booked the photographer. Will you be staying overnight? Only I don't think we can stretch to a hotel."

"What? Oh no, that's all right I have to be back in the evening for a family dinner as my son is back from France."

"Right, well I'll see you tomorrow then."

"Look forward to it," Tavistock replied before disconnecting.

After that she hunted down her debit card and made the reservations, surprised to find that the cheapest option was an Easy Jet flight that day to Gatwick that she could just about make the connections with. Sally, a friend of hers who had a flat in London was rung to see if she could stay overnight and it was only a matter of minutes later that she was packed, in the car and off to the airport. She left a message for Richard and one each for the children and with a feeling of relief arrived at the departure gate with minutes to spare.

★★★

That evening after a very good Italian meal and several bottles of wine shared between Tavistock, her old friend and the latest in a long string of much younger partners she crawled into bed and promptly fell asleep with the date 8th September ringing in her ears.

She awoke in the middle of the night to the smell of damp and coal dust. Stretching out a hand she felt the wet gritty walls of a mean and narrow street. Across the road a woman clearly drunk and desperate was clutching the arm of a man carrying a black bag.

"Come on ducks, I won't charge you much, after all yus a

genelman an' all."

"But ..." the man remonstrated, trying to disentangle himself. The woman grabbed him around the waist and leant in, breathing a mixture of raw onion and raw alcohol into his face. He recoiled and pushed her up against the wall.

"That's all right dearie, I likes 'em rough." She grinned back at him.

"But ... look," he hissed, looking almost fearfully around. "You have to go now, it's not safe."

"Oh don't be such a spoilsport," she laughed.

"Yes, don't be such a spoilsport Jack." Tavistock watched in growing dismay as a figure emerged from behind the half-open gate which appeared to block the entrance of a dark and silent yard.

"Well my love, if he doesn't want to avail himself of your services I certainly do."

"It'll cost you," she replied, leaning against the wall; one shoulder peeked nakedly from underneath her tattered shawl and she thrust out her ample and wrinkled breasts in what she believed was a provocative fashion. On a much younger woman it may have been alluring but on her Tavistock found it almost embarrassing in its desperation.

"Of course. Jack, give her some money." Jack thrust his hand into his coat pocket and handed her a few coins.

She looked at the coins and then at the two men and shrugged.

"All right but if you both want a go it's extra. An' I'm only accepting this as you're so young and handsome," she announced, archly looking into the eyes of the man now standing beside her.

"Come on," he said, holding out his hand, "I've found a nice quiet place where we won't be disturbed." Grinning at his silent companion Jack he led her towards the gate and into the small yard behind. In a dim corner he had laid sacking on the ground in preparation and the woman's eyes widened slightly. Beside the sacking was a lamp such as miners used, its light harsh and white.

"I usually works in the dark," she muttered, suddenly afraid and growing soberer with each stride that she made further into the yard.

"If you're frightened of onlookers don't be, the surrounding properties are mostly abandoned or only used during the day and those that are lived in have no windows that look down into this particular spot. I chose it deliberately."

"But why the lamp?" she hissed back at him.

"Oh because our friend Jack there likes to watch."

"Oh, I thought 'e wos a shy one." She giggled and threw Jack a coy and duplicitous look.

"Yes, let's just say it will be an education for him." He smiled confidingly down at her and pressed his hand into her heaving cleavage. "Close the gate, Jack," He ordered as she obediently lay down and pushed up her skirts. Tavistock who had followed them in watched in growing horror as the younger of the two fumbled with the woman's clothing and then sat astride her ample legs.

"Well," she muttered growing nervous, "get on with it, it's bleedin' cold."

The man leant in as if to kiss her and then with a swift and lightning flash of silver sunk the knife into her exposed stomach and with a deft twist pulled the blade down from below her breast to her navel. The scream of pain and shock was stopped as his companion raced over and covered her mouth with his hands. Her eyes stared up at him and she struggled desperately as the pain managed to make itself felt despite the amount of alcohol she had consumed that night.

The contents of her stomach spilled out in a wave of

steaming fluid and glistening intestines. Blood flowed across her clothing and between her legs.

Jack held onto her head and hissed at his master. " For pity's sake end this. I know she's only a pox-ridden doxy but even they don't deserve to die like this."

His master looked up and grinned back at him, plainly enjoying the kill.

"Besides she's making too much noise and someone will hear her before you finish."

"Oh very well Jack," the younger of the two muttered as with reluctance he turned and with two swift and solid cuts almost severed the woman's neck and as he did Jack saw with relief that the light died from their victim's eyes.

"And now I will find the uterus and remove it. I think that it should be here. Yes see. And now it is clearly exposed."

Jack got up and moved towards the gate; he felt sick and shaken and the worst of it was that the boy appeared to be enjoying himself if the bulge in his trousers was anything to go by.

Tavistock stood beside him and watched as he tried desperately to light his pipe.

Eventually he was joined by his young master who handed him back the money he had reluctantly paid the woman.

"What's that?" Jack pointed out as he watched his young employer pocketing something that shone dimly in the gloom.

"Oh just a couple of rings."

"You stole her wedding band?" Jack exclaimed with shock.

"And the keeper. Oh stop looking at me like that, she won't be needing them and I'd like something to remind me of this night's work."

"But ..." Jack's eyes turned to the leather bag in which

the uterus had been thrust and shuddered. "Why keep any of it?"

"What, this? Of no use now but it will give the police a shock to find it missing. I'll dispose of it in the boiler room when we get back. I need to throw in my clothes as well, and so do you. Don't worry, I'll buy you new ones."

Jack watched almost fascinated, as did Tavistock, as the lantern was dimmed and the gate closed behind them as they left and Tavistock felt herself fading into the darkening night, the scents and sounds dimming as she struggled to escape the clutches of wine and sleep.

She awoke with a start and turned on her bedside light, the alarm clock beside her glowed blue and in its reassuring modern glow she could clearly see that the time was ten to six. Ten minutes before the body of Annie Chapman was discovered in the early hours of Saturday 8th September 1888.

Tavistock was still trying to forget what she had seen when she walked into Daunts Bookshop a little before noon that day and asked to see the manager. A tall man emerged from behind a tower of books and informed her that he was the manager.

"Great." said Tavistock. "I'm Tavistock Allan."

The man looked momentarily puzzled and then suddenly smiled down at her.

"The writer."

"Yes. Um, where do you want me to sit?"

"Sit?"

"Yes for the signing and I think there was to be a reading as well."

"Reading?" he repeated, clearly puzzled.

"Yes reading, only I can't see any books out so I presume it's to be in another part of the shop," Tavistock informed him.

"I'm really, really sorry but I have absolutely no idea what you are talking about."

"But your assistant rang me yesterday and said that the person you had booked for today couldn't make it and would I fill in?"

"My assistant. Not Miss Neville?"

"No it was a man. He sounded young, if that's any help."

"I don't suppose he gave you his name?"

Tavistock frowned. "No. Actually now I come to think of it he never did."

"Oh." He gave her the smallest of kindly smiles, the kind of smile that pre-empted the buttoning-up of the little white coat with many buckles.

"And so you dropped everything to come here because a strange man rang and asked you to come?"

"Yes."

The man watched her as her face fell and was suddenly aware that she was also shaking slightly.

"Look, I'm very sorry about this but I'm afraid that someone has played a rather nasty trick on you."

"I see."

"I'd really like you to do a reading at some point, I mean we do have all your books, even the ones not now in print." He pointed to a far corner of the shop to illustrate his point and on seeing her blank expression added, "perhaps I could arrange something nearer Christmas, say November, when our in-house book club has its regular guest speaker?"

"That would be great." Tavistock smiled back at him while telling herself to pull it all together.

"Look, would you like a coffee or something?"

"No, no, it's fine, I'll just go and have a walk for a while, see the sights. Make the most of a day off in London."

"Are you sure that you're okay?" he asked, not quite

believing her.

"Yes, positive. I'm absolutely fine. Well it's a wonderful place you have here," Tavistock observed, looking around. "And it will be great to come back and sign for real," she added, meaning every word.

Relieved that she wasn't about to either faint or have a screaming tantrum the manager pottered off to a counter containing a small till and a computer and after punching in a code turned and said, "Yes that's a definite, I'll contact your publisher and organise something. Now if you could just give me the contact details I'll email them today and start the ball rolling."

"I have a card somewhere with my editor's details on ..." Tavistock rummaged in her handbag and after a brief hiatus extracted a small card and handed it over. "Best to ring her after the first caffeine shot at ten."

"Right."

Tavistock smiled again and held out her hand. He shook it and then turning smartly on her heel, Tavistock walked out and marched off down the road. An hour later she found herself in Whitechapel High Street. She had very little idea as to how she had got there but now that she was she would take advantage of the opportunity and go and find if the places she had been seeing in her dreams were still around. There was a small coffee shop ahead of her and after equipping herself with a map of the area from the newsagents next door and purchasing a takeaway Americano she headed off in the direction of Mitre Square.

***

A little later Tavistock sat on a park bench and surveyed an area of tree and pavement and felt surprisingly glad that very few of the murder sites were actually still the same, or at least if they were she couldn't find them. Musing on the quirks of life she glanced down at her watch and realised that she had better get going and head back to the airport to catch her flight home. The mix-up was still a little upsetting but not, she told herself, quite as much as that stupid dream.

***

At the same moment as she sat contemplating on her bench a door in a modern Docklands flat was flung open and the woman who had answered the door was pushed to the ground. A knife was thrust into her abdomen and twisted, her anguished scream cut off as her assailant pulled the knife out and then with a motion so swift that the blade was nothing more than a blur of silver severed her carotid artery and then to make sure, sliced her neck open in the other direction. After she was completely still he painstakingly removed the uterus and pushed it down the waste disposal in the kitchen sink. He then stepped out of the shoes he had bought that day and the long plastic rain mac and putting them both in a backpack, let himself out after carefully dropping a couple of long dark hairs in the blood congealing against the door.

Later as he waited for his flight he crossed another name off the list and watched as Tavistock Allan walked into the departure lounge and sat down opposite him.

Chapter 22

Brian Clague had not had a good morning. His immediate superior was furious at the fuss caused by him interviewing Tavistock and had passed the anger from his superior down the food chain. So it was not in a happy or even helpful mood that he answered the call from an opposite number in the Met.

"Brian, it's Tim Corkhill here."

"Tim – good grief, talk about a blast from the past, what do you want?"

"Always a man who goes to straight to the heart of things, eh?" Tim laughed and then was immediately serious.

"Look I know this sounds a bit bizarre but I've just attended a crime scene and apart from the fact that it turned my stomach, it's come up as a match on HOLMES with a scene you attended not long ago."

Brian felt a horrible sinking feeling in his chest and found that his hand was shaking.

"Banker with his throat cut until it's almost severed and a horrible wound in the abdomen?" Brian asked, holding his breath.

"Ditto, only this time the uterus was removed and then pushed down the waste disposal unit."

"You're kidding me!"

"No, only wish I was. And the worst thing is that the abdominal injury was made before the throat was severed."

"And your victim was a banker?"

"One of those high-flying, very highly paid investment bankers. I've done a spot of digging and she was a colleague of your missing banker Oliver Mandrake.

"Anything left at the scene, any witnesses, CCTV coverage?"

"Nothing much so far except two long brown hairs found in the blood of the victim which was odd as the victim was a silver blonde. Only person to see her before she was killed was her cleaner who said she was waiting for someone and seemed excited about it. She also said that as she was leaving the apartment block someone bumped into her on the way in. She described that person as of being of medium height, long brown hair, blue raincoat and a bright scarf with peacock feathers on it. She noticed the scarf as it was one that looked expensive and she has a thing for scarves."

"Did she notice anything else?"

"No … Well only that the person who bumped into her had plenty of room to avoid her but appeared to be in a rush and was wearing a perfume she recognised."

"Which one?"

"Daisy by Mark Jacobs, she knows because her daughter always wants a bottle for Christmas."

Something in the back of Brian's brain went click and he felt suddenly cold and rather sick.

"Are you sure that the witness definitely saw this person."

"Oh yes, and she also noticed that our suspect used the lift and that it stopped at the victim's floor."

"How did she notice that?"

"She was changing out of her work shoes into trainers and

was standing by the lift at the time."

"So no missing that then."

"No."

"How long before anyone raised the alarm?"

"One of the neighbours came back from the shops and saw the blood seeping under the victim's front door about a quarter of an hour later and we were called in. Which was a bit of luck really as the cleaner wasn't expected back until after the weekend."

"Anybody caught on camera leaving?"

"Only one, long hair and a long coat and scarf with some sort of pattern on it matching the description of the witness. Although it appears to be wearing clothes not covered in blood, which you would've expected. Thought you ought to be informed because frankly the murder mirrors your victim."

"Thanks Tim. Look, can you send me any results you get from forensics and I'll send you all the stuff we have here? You never know, we might just get lucky and find a common denominator."

"Um … Brian?"

"Yes."

"Well this sounds a bit nuts and I admit that saying it out loud really scares the crap out of me but I've been googling the old Ripper stories and, well, both of our victims are dead ringers for the original first two victims Mary Ann Nichols and …"

"Annie Chapman," Brian interjected.

"I note that your victim was killed on the 31st August."

"And yours was killed today, 8th September."

"So basically we may have a serial killer knocking off bankers in the style of Jack the Ripper."

"My cup runneth over."

"And mine."

They both sighed in unison as visions of the amount of paperwork and the number of rampant reporters who would be on the story like a pack of vampiric wolves after a two-week fast hit both policemen at the same time.

"My Chief Constable is going nuts," Brian admitted miserably. "We don't get many murders over here and we certainly don't ever get them like this."

"I'd like to say the same but even for London cutting someone open, taking out their uterus and then flushing it down the sink is decidedly over the top," Tim muttered as he doodled on the notepad in front of him.

They both sat in silence hundreds of miles apart and both said at exactly the same time.

"When's the next one due?"

Both launched themselves at their respective computers. Brian got to the answer first though as it was already in his history page.

"According to Wikipedia on the 30th September we will have two more," he advised with a frown.

"Two. Are you sure?" Tim asked as the Wikipedia page came to life on his computer. "Ah, I see he was disturbed during the third murder and so went and found someone else, the sick little puppy."

'Yep, basically we have less than a month to catch the bugger."

"Less than a month with almost no forensic evidence, no witnesses and no motive that anyone can think of and that's if he sticks to the old timescale and for some reason doesn't accelerate the killing."

"And the only common link is that they are both bankers and that they both knew Oliver Mandrake."

"It's something I suppose. Look, I'll head over to the fraud and general nerd department and see if we have anything on

Oliver Mandrake. I don't suppose you could pull him in and I could come over and interview the bastard?"

"Sorry, I'd love to see you using the thumbscrews and desk lamp but unfortunately Mr Mandrake went missing at the same time as we found our first victim and those circumstances came with great pools of blood. Unfortunately we still don't have a body to go with the blood."

"Pity."

"Still, look on the bright side, we have about three weeks to come up with something."

"Piece of cake then."

"Yeah, a piece of cake." They could both feel the mutual grin spreading from one to the other down the telephone line and with that happy thought both of them disconnected and then as reality hit looked miserably around their respective desks. 'I'm a dead man walking,' each thought, and then galvanised, Tim went off to have a word with a friend who dealt solely with dodgy bankers while Brian picked up the phone and rang Richard Allan.

He was put through almost immediately.

"I hope this is a bloody apology, Brian," Richard barked, only barely holding on to his temper.

"Not exactly," Brian replied.

"Well what do you want now?"

"I was just wondering if Tavistock has a long black or dark blue raincoat."

"A raincoat?" Richard repeated.

"And a scarf, say a bright blue one with peacock feathers."

"Well yes, as it happens, her sister gave it to her for a birthday present. Think she picked it up from Harvey Nicks. I know that it must have cost a small fortune and Tavistock always wears it for signings, says it brings her luck."

"Yeah, I thought I remembered her wearing it for a reading

at Douglas Town Library last Christmas."

"Brian, just exactly what is going on?"

"I'm not sure. Look, could I speak to Tavistock at home do you think, without her wanting to do horrible things to me?"

"No, sorry she can't."

"Oh."

"Not because she wouldn't like to do foul things to your good self but because she's not here."

Brian suddenly had an odd feeling and looking again at the screen in front of him almost whispered "Please tell me she's not off the Island."

"Well yes, as it happens, she left suddenly yesterday and she's in London for some sort of signing. One of those big independents."

"I don't suppose you can remember which one?"

"Yes it was the same name as one of our old ... Daunts, that's it ... Daunts. She was really pleased actually, said it would make a nice change to be back in a civilised country where they don't disembowel members of the finance sector."

Brian laughed miserably, "Um, I wouldn't be too sure about that."

"Is everything all right? I mean I'm sorry I shouted but she is my wife, however odd she might get when she's into a book and anyway she's promised no more Ripper stuff."

"Right." Brian doodled a large knife on the notepad in front of him before asking as nonchalantly as he was able, "Don't suppose she's coming back tonight?"

"As a matter of fact yes. She should be back by six, as George is back from France for a week or so and we are off to the Portofino for a celebratory dinner."

"Look, can you ask her to give me a ring when she gets in? I'll give you my mobile number. And Richard don't forget, this is really, really important. Really important."

"Fine. I'll get her to ring you before we go out."

"Good. Well I'll ... er ... see you soon at some point no doubt."

"Not if I can help it," Richard muttered as he replaced the telephone and went back to the report he had been reading.

***

Brian sat and looked at the papers in front of him and then after getting the telephone number from directory enquiries rang the London Bookshop. There were a number of Daunts Bookshops and he got lucky with the second number.

"Yes this is Daunts Bookshop, the manager speaking, how may I help you?"

"Um ... actually this may sound a little mad but did a writer called Tavistock Allan turn up at your bookshop today?"

"Well yes, she did."

"Oh good, what time did she get there?"

"About twelve."

"Great."

"I'm sorry but did you say great?"

"Yes, yes I did."

"And may I enquire why?" The voice had gone from warmly charming to icy.

"Because a signing takes time doesn't it? I mean by the time you've done a reading or two and the Q&A is never less than half an hour, plus the signing itself and even if it's only a signing that's never usually less than two hours otherwise it wouldn't be worth getting the books in." Brian came to a sudden halt as he belatedly recognised the frost at the other end of the line.

"Look young man, I have no idea why you should think this is funny but frankly playing a practical joke like that on a very nice lady is pretty despicable."

"Joke?"

"As if you didn't know!"

Brian, nonplussed, stared at his computer screen as the voice continued to get colder.

"You know damn well that there was no signing. Mrs Allan left somewhat upset, even though she very bravely tried not to show it, about ten minutes after twelve."

"Oh God," Brian breathed.

"What, what did you say?"

"Are you absolutely sure that she left at that time?"

"Of course I'm sure. It's not something I would make up, unlike some people I could mention."

"I'm sorry?"

"And so you should be." And with that the manager hung up leaving Brian in a state of shock before he could explain who he was.

There had been no signing, and looking at the timeline that Tim had sent him by email together with a map of the area where the victim had lived, Tavistock could very well have gone to the flat, murdered the unfortunate Izobelle Du Maurier and still had time to catch her plane back.

"I need good old Uncle Bob," Brian thought, "and I need him now."

Chapter 23

Bob and Brian sat inside The Velvet Lobster and sipped on their respective beverages. Brian had relayed all the information that Tim had given him to his old boss and then watched almost with relief as Bob's devious brain went into overdrive.

"And why are you telling me all of this?" Bob asked him as his little grey cells sprung into action..

"Because you used to go through people's bins looking for evidence and without a search warrant and you nearly always got your man despite your unorthodox methods. Besides which, as a well-respected member of the private sector you can resort to methods which would have me up against the wall in the ACC's office with a list of charges and disciplinary actions against my name a mile long."

"True, very true, my young apprentice."

"Anyway the more I think about it, the more it looks like a set-up."

"You now think as I do that someone is trying to frame Tavistock?"

"Yes." Brian paused and looked deep into his coffee mug. "The thing I don't understand is why."

"Odd."

"Very." They sat in silence for a few seconds, a silence broken by Brian. "She'll get off. I mean she couldn't possibly have done any of it."

"That's not what you said ..."

"Yes I know it wasn't, but I was tired and cross and desperate. But now I can clearly see that someone is tampering with the evidence and deliberately laying down breadcrumbs."

"And it all boils down to our missing banker."

"I think so, yes."

"Leave it with me young Brian, at least overnight. I'll have a word with Clive, see if we can find anything from our own tapes on the Mandrakes and with our ... er ... consultant and I'll get back to you."

"Consultant?"

"Walks through walls, that sort of thing."

"Oh him, well good luck with that then."

Brian finished his drink, ate the last of his doughnut and then toddled off towards his car parked at the side of his new office. Bob sat and finished his decaf, low fat drink and after a few minutes turned in the opposite direction and made his way up Prospect Hill towards the government offices and the little room in the basement where his quarry usually lurked.

***

He arrived just as Barty was about to lock up for the day after having made a not insubstantial amount of money on his favourite internet gaming site.

"Is the boss about?" Bob asked.

"In there," Barty answered, nodding at a firmly closed door.

Bob knocked and on hearing a reply entered to find Mannanan Mac Lir trying to hit a small golf ball into a white plastic party cup.

"Not interrupting anything important, am I?" Bob asked with only a trace of sarcasm in his voice.

"Shh," Mannanan replied as he hit the ball with a gentle phut sound and it slowly dribbled across the carpet and into the waiting receptacle. Mannanan grinned broadly and putting his metal putter aside, went back to his desk, sat down in his large leather wing chair and after extracting a bottle of Balvenie from one drawer in his desk and two small glasses from another, filled both and passed one over to Bob, who had slumped almost with relief into the other chair.

"Thanks," Bob muttered, taking a long pull of his drink. "I actually really needed that."

"Think nothing of it and before you ask this delightful malt is entirely fat free." Mannanan advised with a wicked grin.

"Good. At least something is."

"So what brings you to my humble and inadequately heated lair?" Mannanan asked after they had both settled into their respective seats and the whisky had begun to spread its urbane warmth through them both.

"It's Tavistock."

"What is?"

"She's in trouble. A lot of trouble."

"Are you sure? I mean normally she calls to me when she needs help and I've heard nothing."

"Thing is, she doesn't actually know that she's in deep and serious. At least not until the knock on the door and the police drag her off to help with their enquiries."

"Oh come now Bob, it can't be that bad. Besides Brian wouldn't let them."

"It's Brian and his little wizards who will be doing the dragging and the way things stand I hope that Richard can get a really good criminal lawyer. Both here and across."

"Across? Good God – what on earth do they think she has done?"

"They think that she has finally done one too many digs into the murky underworld of the past and has murdered two or possibly three investment bankers, Ripper-style with a knife she thinks may have belonged to Jack the Ripper."

"But …"

"Let me finish, it gets worse. She has absolutely no alibi for the times of either killing. She could very easily have been in both places. Brian sent me a copy of an email from a mate in London and they have CCTV pictures of someone who looks a lot like Tavistock, wearing a scarf that is a dead ringer for one she is always known to wear, entering and leaving a building just before and just after a woman was killed in fairly horrible circumstances. They also now apparently have a link to both victims and Tavistock met them both at a reception last year. The only evidence found at the second scene were two long brown hairs and I would put ready money on the fact that when tested they will in fact belong to Tavistock. Somebody is setting one of my oldest and best friends up for murder and unfortunately the only one who can possibly help is you."

"Me?"

"Yes, you."

"Oh."

"We have twenty-one days before the next two earmarked to die meet a really horrible end and whatever case this sociopath is building up against Tavistock comes to a head."

"Not a lot of time then."

"The next original Ripper murders were about half an hour apart and both occurred on the morning of Sunday the 30th September. We have no idea who the next victims are and no idea where they are going to die but I bet you anything you like that Tavistock will somehow be in the thick of it."

"Umm, I'm not so sure. I also know someone with long brown hair, someone who has far better links to dear old Jack."

"Really, who?"

"Nobody you would know my dear Bob, and no one you need to talk to either. In fact I think you can safely leave the rest to me and then you can't possibly be accused of interfering." Mannanan took a long sip of his drink and then looked covertly over the rim of his glass towards the worried form of Bob Callow. "Just one thing, these cameras of yours, they do, I suspect, cover most things even if strictly speaking they don't belong to you?"

"Well, yes," Bob replied with a shrug.

"Good."

"Why?"

"I want you to go back to the beginning and look at the life and works of our missing banker. Think about him as you would that delightfully amusing cartoon character Wally."

"You don't mean the chap in the red and white stripy hat, 'Where's Wally'?"

"Exactly, only in this particular case it will be a matter of 'Where's Olly?' Don't worry, you'll see what I mean when you find him." And with that enigmatic statement Mannanan vanished, taking both his glass and the whisky bottle with him.

Chapter 24

"So I can have it back?" Tavistock asked as Brian sat opposite her and handed over the knife he had previously confiscated.

Brian looked at the expression on her face and then at the horn-handled blade he was holding still encased in a plastic evidence bag.

"Don't you want it back?" he asked.

Tavistock looked up at him and then back at the bag. "To be honest I'm not really sure. The damn thing has been nothing but trouble since I got it."

"Trouble?"

"I've been having bad dreams, really weird ones since it came into the house."

"Not about the Ripper?"

Tavistock threw him a look and then stood up.

"I suppose it isn't really surprising considering what I was thinking about writing, anyway thanks for bringing it back."

"No hard feelings?" Brian asked a trifle nervously.

"Has Dear Old Uncle Bob been getting at you?" Tavistock asked him with a grin.

"A bit, he can use very colourful language now he's in the private sector."

"I know," Tavistock replied with feeling, remembering her last conversation in which Bob Callow had described her jaunt to London in terms even her own children wouldn't have used.

"Still, we have the entire board of Wilson, Hansard and DeLouche, or what's left of it, under protective custody. Mandrake's family are still being watched over by good old Uncle Bob and the forensic report on the knife is clean. Well I say clean but according to the boffins the blood caught up between the handle and the blade is extremely old and a mixture of animal and human."

"Animal?" Tavistock looked at him in alarm as she remembered one of the earlier dreams and the scene down at the loch. She shuddered and dropped the knife on the table in front of her.

Brian picked the weapon up and blithely carried on. "Deer, they think. I mean that would make sense as it's a hunting knife. Problem is the human blood.It's not just even one or two blood groups but all of them, which doesn't make a lot of sense unless … "

"It really was Jack the Ripper's knife."

"What!" Brian looked down at the thing in his hand with horror and hastily dumped it back on the polished coffee table in front of them.

"You don't …" his voice tailed off and then he saw the twinkle in her eye and laughed aloud in relief. "Good one Mrs Allan, you nearly got me there."

Tavistock grinned back at him, she had her own views on the knife in question but had begun to realise that she would be best to keep them to herself for the time being.

"Everyone knows he used a cut-throat razor, eh," Brian stated, remembering some of the theories he had recently read online.

"Or maybe a scalpel."

"You think he may have been a medical student?"

"Possibly. I've been doing a bit of digging and they always suspected that the *Dear Boss* letter purporting to come from Jack the Ripper was written by a medical student."

"The *Dear Boss* letter?" Brian sat back and accepted another mug of coffee from the cafetiere in front of them. After helping him to milk and sugar Tavistock got up and left the room returning a few minutes later with a brownish piece of paper covered in red writing.

"There you go." Tavistock handed him the square of paper and returned to her seat. "Written on the 25th September, or at least dated the 25th if we are to be strictly accurate as it was actually postmarked 27th September 1888. It was received that day by the Central News Agency who sent it on to Scotland Yard. Scotland Yard received it on the 29th but it wasn't until Elizabeth Stride and Catherine Eddowes were found dead on the morning of the 30th September that they took any notice."

Brian, who had been trying to decipher the handwriting, looked up. "It says here that he intends to clip the lady's ears off and send to the police officers. Did he?"

"On that point there is a bit of a debate. The ear was clipped or rather nicked but it wasn't severed or sent anywhere. The police thought it was a hoax. Thing is, look at the writing and the deliberate spelling mistakes. Doesn't look to me like an uneducated writer."

"Hmm. Medical student. So they didn't find a suspect amongst the students they interviewed then."

"No."

"Not one?" Brian asked in surprise.

"Not a single one, mainly because they never interviewed any of them. It was thought not to be the done thing. After all they might have upset all those powerful influence-wielding parents, and besides it was only prostitutes who were being killed so it had to be someone of the same ilk who killed them."

"What!"

"Political correctness is not a new thing Brian, it was just called a different name then."

"Oh."

"It was called the class system. Take the Crimean War for instance: before Florence Nightingale turned up the common soldier was not allowed chloroform before they amputated as he was a man and could take the pain. Even after she arrived it was months before she could actually distribute clean shirts and blankets. Thousands of men died in terrible circumstances just because they weren't officers but members of the lower classes and therefore not people and certainly not one of them in inverted commas!"

"I know she did a lot for nursing, brought hospitals out of the dark ages."

"Bet you didn't know about her reforms though."

"You mean nursing reforms?"

"Yep, and there was one in particular which really got up the nose of the middle and upper classes."

"What?"

"She wanted them to recognise that prostitutes had rights to both medical and social care."

"And they didn't?"

"Oh God no. Prostitutes, doxies, whores whatever you like to call them had no rights, they were non-people and what they did was their own fault. Even if their husbands had left them if they had ever had one, and they had no other means of supporting themselves."

"And of course their services were never used by anyone

from the upper or middle class," Brian added.

"Exactly."

"So Jack could have been a medical student and not a minor member of royalty."

"My thoughts exactly. Mind you there were hundreds of suspects, probably thousands down the years."

"Why did he stop?" Brian asked, handing the letter back, intrigued despite himself.

"I think he died that or he qualified and no longer needed to practise for his anatomy exam."

"Another doctor killing off the surplus population."

"Quite. Anyway enough of the old, what's new in the investigation, as I presume I'm no longer a suspect?"

"Cleared on all counts, especially as we have a witness or two who saw you on a park bench miles away from the murder site at the same time as the murderer was entering the building. Oh and the hairs we found, long and brown, weren't yours. But it does appear that someone is trying to set you up."

"Who?"

"I want you to take a look at this." Brian opened up his laptop which had until that point been quietly sitting on the table beside him and after a few moment clicked a button and pushed it over towards Tavistock. The screen had frozen on a single frame of a film of various people in what was clearly some sort of waiting area.

"That's London City Airport departure lounge."

"Yes on the day you came back, the day of the murder. Recognise anyone?"

"No – I ..." Tavistock watched as Brian clicked another button and people came and went. A face she recognised passed almost in profile and Tavistock gasped. "Brian – stop it there and run it back a bit."

Brian did as he was asked and Tavistock stared at the screen in mounting horror.

"That woman, there the one in the dark brown coat. I know her, she's Clara Callister. An old schoolfriend. I met her some time ago as she's come back to the Island and I've had lunch with her. She knows all about my having to stop writing the Ripper book."

"And she has long brown hair. She also lives in a small cottage just above the house your Kate was showing a prospective buyer round."

"But it doesn't make any sense. I mean why would she set me up? We hadn't had anything to do with each other for years before we met up recently."

"That's what I'd like to know."

"Can I keep a copy of this?"

"I suppose so. I can email it to you."

"Can you do it now?"

"Sure, why?"

"Because …" Tavistock frowned down at the screen with murder plainly on her mind. Brian cleared his throat and made a tentative suggestion.

"I'm unofficially going up to see Clara today with our mutual friend Bob, bit unorthodox I know but you could come too if you like?"

"When?"

"Now."

"I'll get my coat."

A second or so after Tavistock and Brian had departed from Tavistock's house, in a flurry of beech chippings and a squeal of tyres, as Brian just about avoided Tavistock's old and decrepit cat who had taken to sleeping in the sun in the middle of the drive's entrance, Mannanan Mac Lir emerged from the dust motes caught in the sunlight streaming through the big bay windows of the lounge and turned to glare at his companion.

"I thought, Barty, that when I asked you to keep an eye on young Clara you would actually do so."

"But I did."

"I followed her off Island, I even went on a train for the first time in years and I trawled around London with her. And may I say Boss that at no time did I see her slit someone's throat or disembowel them."

"Did she visit anyone, anyone at all?"

"She met a woman for lunch."

"Oh, and what did they do?"

"Well they had a sort of soup and then a steak with French fries and wilted spinach and for dessert they …"

"Barty, I meant what did they say?"

"The woman, Izobelle something said that she hadn't heard from Olly somebody and Clara told her to let her know when she did. Oh and they talked about some guy who had fallen under a train."

"Why?"

"Well Clara seemed to think that this Martin had had something to do with her husband's death."

"And then what?"

"Well they exchanged hugs and then Clara went shopping."

"Shopping?"

"She bought a new laptop and some card things with programmes on and a couple of cameras."

"What would she need more than one camera for?"

"I have no idea. They were really small and the guy in the place she had bought them said you could put them in anything. She also bought a tub of Pringles and a can of Coke."

"Why?"

“Well I thought she was hungry at first but as she bought them both in the place where she got the cameras, who knows?”

“Ummm.”

“So what do we do now, Boss?”

“We go and sit in on this meeting of Brian’s.”

“Why?”

“Because I have a horrible feeling that it’s not Tavistock who is the target of our resourceful killer, but Clara. And Clara is one of our own, Barty, one of our own.”

Chapter 25

Bob, Brian and Tavistock met at the bottom of the old road leading up to Clara's cottage and viewed the narrow bramble-edged lane with a joint sigh. Both Brian and Bob had arrived in their own vehicles and neither was happy about driving their car up the potholed and deeply rutted track. They were about to head up on foot when Mannanan and Barty emerged before them.

"I wouldn't bother if I were you," Mannanan advised them, looking cross and frustrated.

"She's not there, hasn't been for a couple of days now."

"Well where the hell is she?" Brian asked.

"I have no idea. Barty, you were supposed to be looking after her."

They all as one turned and glared at the offending ghost who was beginning to fade into the surrounding hedgerow.

"Oh no you don't," muttered Mannanan, grabbing his sleeve.

"Look boss I did as you said," Barty wheedled. "I followed her all around London, I even went on that horrible plane and the last time I saw her she was here, unpacking her shopping and drinking gin."

"And when was that?"

"Last night, no tell a lie it was the night before last, and she hasn't left the Island because the alarm in the office would have gone off."

"Then where can she have gone? And why does the place look and feel so empty?"

"Dunno Boss."

Tavistock, who had been frowning up to that point, suddenly had a thought.

"Did she have the dogs with her?"

Barty frowned in concentration and then remembered. "No, now that I come to think of it, that's odd, I mean she dropped them off at her friend's place a couple of days ago.. Then she spent a lot of time in that internet café on Victoria Street. Oh and she went to a travel agents several times."

"What!" they all exclaimed.

Before, however, Barty could be questioned further they all heard the sound of an elderly vehicle grinding towards them from the direction of the road below.

Tavistock turned and with a relieved shout of, "That's her," pointed to the oncoming vehicle which hooted its horn at them as it continued slowly upwards.

"We'd better get out of the way," Bob advised, jumping up and onto the ledge of grass-covered earth edging the sunken roadway. "I doubt she can stop until she gets to that turning place near the cottage. And if she does stop she may not be able to get it to start again!"

Tavistock and Brian followed suit and Mannanan and Barty vanished to reappear a minute later as the mud-spattered Land Rover passed them by in a haze of churned-up dirt and loose stones. They all hurried up the lane after her and reached Clara just as she was extracting her dogs from the boot.

"And to what do I owe this dubious house call?" Clara

asked, rescuing a bag of groceries from the foot well. The dogs bounded around her visitors until she called them to order and after opening the front door ushered them all inside.

After she had applied a match to the carefully pre-laid fire and put the kettle on she returned to her own lounge with a tray of tea, coffee, biscuits and an assortment of oddly matched mugs. Outside the small snug cottage the wind began to moan and howl followed by a sudden squally shower of heavy rain.

When they had all settled in various chairs including a couple dragged from behind her small dining table. Clara picked up her mug and looking over the rim, fixed her gaze on Tavistock.

"Well," she declared, "what do you want and why have you brought the burly back-up, to say nothing of involving rent-a-ghost and Caspar?"

Barty was about to remonstrate as was Brian when Tavistock, who had been glaring at Clara, banged her mug down on the table in front of them and shouted. "What do I want? You really don't know?"

"No," Clara replied, reason personified, "I really don't."

"What I want," Tavistock hissed through clenched teeth, "is to know just why you are trying to frame me for two murders I know damn well that *I* didn't commit."

"Oh Tavistock old friend," Clara sighed, sadly putting down her drink. "I'm not trying to frame you but I have a horrible feeling that someone is trying to frame me. I'm also pretty certain that he has at least three more people on his list that he is going to despatch and there is nothing I can do about it, although God knows I've tried. I mean I went and saw Izobelle and warned her, I told her not to talk to him."

"But you were there at the airport terminal, you were stalking me."

"Actually I was doing my damnedest to avoid you. Anyway

how do you know?"

"Brian showed me a tape, go on Brian, show her," Tavistock demanded, sitting back with her arms tightly folded across her chest and a look of utter disbelief on her face.

Brian, who had been about to say something, hesitated and then produced the laptop he had been carrying in a small backpack and set it up. After a brief hiatus Clara watched as he replayed the tape. She was clearly visible and as the camera caught her it also caught another face, only just visible in a corner seat.

"Stop!" she shouted with excitement.

Brian pressed pause and she stabbed at the figure with her index finger.

"That's him, the little shit, that's ..."

"Wally," Bob muttered in amazement.

"Wally?" Brian, Clara and Tavistock repeated.

"Wally, I mean Olly. That's Oliver Mandrake, my missing banker and the little sod is very obviously not dead, he doesn't even look particularly ill, a medical miracle considering the amount of blood he was presumed to have lost." Bob chortled, grinning at Mannanan who was leaning over Brian to get a better look.

"Barty," Mannanan asked, "have you ever seen this man?"

"Yes Boss."

"Where?"

"Well ... er ... here Boss."

"Here!" they all exclaimed.

"Yes, he was waiting round the side of the house where you park your car," he added, looking at Clara.

"He was what!" Mannanan and Clara exploded simultaneously.

"Look, I didn't know that he was public enemy number

one I just thought that he was a lost hiker. I mean he had a map and a backpack and he only stayed a short time before he went."

"And what did he do?"

"Nothing much, he just hung around. Hang on, he did do something a bit odd now what was it?" They waited while he tried to remember and just when Mannanan was about to lose all patience and shake him Barty exclaimed, "He picked stuff up off the ground and put it in a plastic bag."

"What sort of stuff?" Tavistock demanded

"Um stuff from the ground, looked like … well … fur or hairs something like that – you know, stuff."

"Dog hairs," Brian muttered. "Oh shit, but that's bad, I mean it's really bad."

"Why?" Bob asked, "Only I'm beginning to have a very uneasy feeling in the old waters and they are never wrong."

"Me too," Brian replied. "Look, I didn't mention it before because Tavistock was exonerated and she also doesn't have a dog. But forensics found a selection of dog hairs at the scene of the London murder and the victim didn't have any pets. They just assumed that someone had visited her who did."

"Someone like the one who killed her."

"Something like that."

They all sat in a worried silence broken by Tavistock. "So Clara, if I didn't kill them and you didn't, who did? And more importantly, why? Oh and before I forget, why on earth would he do it in the style of Jack the Ripper and then try and blame you?"

"The killer's name is Oliver Mandrake and he is or was my latest client," Bob advised them, getting up.

"So you know?" Clara breathed. "It's not just me going insane."

"Or me." Tavistock grinned back at her.

"Bob, where are you going?" Tavistock asked as Bob moved towards the front door.

"Can't get a good signal here. Before I find out why Clara thinks this creep is doing what he's doing I'm going to call for reinforcements."

"Reinforcements?"

"Yep." And on that single word Bob lifted the latch on the front door and let himself out. He returned a few minutes later grinning broadly and dripping water.

"Still raining I see," Mannanan commented as Bob took his seat by the fire and gently steamed.

"Yep. And in a few minutes, well about half an hour, the Island's finest nose will be sniffing about and with any luck we should find out where Mandrake is hiding out. Because if he's keeping tabs on Clara he must be doing it from somewhere near."

"Hadn't thought of that. My god but you're a devious bugger," Clara breathed.

"Am that, and as we have a bit of time perhaps you could enlighten us as to what is actually going on. As it's the 30th September tomorrow and I'd like if possible to save at least two bankers, although why for the moment escapes me," Bob muttered as an afterthought.

Clara sat back and staring intently into the fire, tried to explain.

"It all started when I realised that my husband hadn't killed himself. Yes I know everyone said he had hung himself while he was depressed over the collapse of his firm. A firm which had been in his family since the reign of Queen Victoria and had managed to survive two World Wars, the Depression and numerous other crises. Couldn't survive the banks though, or rather it could, it just couldn't survive Oliver Mandrake and his board of slimy bastards.

"Thomas, my Thomas, met Oliver or Olly as he liked to be called, at a dinner in London, can't even remember what it was in aid of except that Thomas got completely befuddled on free champagne and ended up ringing me at three in the morning to tell me that he'd had a marvellous new idea to modernise the firm and that the money for the new plant and equipment would be forthcoming, no hassle, as he'd found a willing investor.

"It was just before the recession really bit, just after Northern Rock went down. The firm had been making a small steady profit but not enough to pay for the new machines which Thomas needed because he had the promise of quite a few new orders. Orders that he could fulfil if he had the machines, but he had to have the machinery to get the orders. You see the nasty circle it was causing?"

They all nodded.

"Well with the benefit of hindsight it was a lousy idea and really bad timing but Olly managed to persuade Thomas to borrow the money, in fact Thomas was allowed to borrow a bit more than he needed and that extra bit was the killer. We took out a mortgage on the house and the estate, well basically we hocked everything. Then Thomas found out that the orders weren't going to happen and I've since found out that at least two, the main ones, were never going to happen as they had been made by companies that Oliver and a friend of his already controlled. Offshore companies registered to Oliver and your first victim."

Clara paused as Bob refilled her mug.

"Well, Thomas couldn't pay back the interest let alone the capital he'd borrowed and so he began to sell off what he could. The furniture went first and the paintings his grandfather and his father before him had collected. Only bought us time. In the end Olly turned up wringing his hands and crying crocodile tears, told us he had no option but to foreclose. The plant would be shut down and the administrators would be called in.

"Then a week later just as we had got used to the idea he says that he has a buyer, we won't get much but it will just about let us live, in reduced circumstances of course."

"He?" Bob queried.

"Sorry, Thomas; he said that he had found a buyer and that we'd be all right, a chap he'd known in the trade for some years. I remember him telling me to keep it all a secret and then he came home with a bottle of champagne and we sat in front of the fire and dreamed of buying something really cheap in the sun, miles away from the UK.

"The morning Thomas died he rang me, I was having my hair done and I remember that he sounded excited, he was going to sign the forms that morning. Then he said that Olly was arranging it. My blood ran cold and I decided to get back home, drove like stink and then when I got there it was too late, far too late.

"But I know Thomas didn't commit suicide, the poor sap couldn't tie his own shoelaces let alone a noose which would actually hang anything.

"After that I started asking around really quietly. Found out who might have been involved. Tried to ascertain who the mystery buyer was. No one seemed to know. In fact I have my doubts that there actually was one.

"Made a list. Then started asking them questions. Spoke to Oliver's accountant or his head of accounts as he liked to call himself."

"Martin?" Brian asked.

"Yes. He promised to have a look into it. Said it sounded very like asset-stripping to him, he didn't approve – you could tell. Anyway he said that he'd found something similar in the US accounts and would put them in front of the board. The next day he's conveniently dead and then Olly's Manx Co-Director of the company that was going to give us new business is murdered."

"And Izobelle?" Bob asked.

"A fellow board member of Olly's. She hated Oliver's guts, always thought he was too good to be true. Said she'd seen Oliver pushing something into a bin after one of their board meetings, in fact it had only really come into her head after Martin had died and I asked her about the report. When I last saw her she was going through the computer files, even the deleted ones."

"Then she conveniently dies," Brian murmured.

"There are only three people I now think know more than me about Olly Mandrake and two have disappeared from their homes in Spain and Paris, that's where I've been by the way. Had to go by ferry, train and then Eurotunnel. After the one in Spain wasn't there I just flew home. As for the last name, well he won't take my calls and I can't get near him.

"Tomorrow is the 30th September and I'm absolutely convinced that two of them will die and the only evidence you will find will be from me."

The others who had sat and listened in growing horror gave a collective gasp as she finished; by then the cottage was so quiet that when a log fell from the fire they all jumped as one.

"Do you have the list?" Brian asked.

"Here," Clara muttered, reaching across to the handbag that she had discarded by her seat, and extracted from its chunky depths a thin slip of paper.

"Lydia Spike, Karl Murray and Noel Hansard," Brian read aloud and then got out his laptop and went online.

"How are you doing that?" Clara asked. "I mean this place

doesn't have internet access."

"Ah that's because this little toy is a complete tart and manages to attach itself to anything within miles, direct link to the stars as it were. Ah here we go. Right I've made my request and with any luck I should have a reply within, if not minutes, well a few hours."

"So what do I do now?" Clara asked.

"Nothing," Brian replied with a smile. "You've done all the legwork so now you can leave it all to us."

At that moment there was a bang on the door.

Bob leapt up to answer it and to usher in a rather damp Pete and an enormous dog.

"No! Don't even think about it," Pete shouted as Mr Pickles went straight for the plate of biscuits, tail wagging and lips drooling. Clara's dogs, who had been sprawled in front of the fire looked up in alarm and then hid behind her armchair.

Clara, who had a soft spot for anything canine, rushed to his defence.

"Oh just one can't hurt. I mean, look at the size of him. He needs to keep his strength up, don't you boy?" she crooned, fondling his ears as he sat at her feet and dribbled onto the carpet.

"He can have one afterwards," Pete groaned. "And as for you, you hairy big manipulating softie, it's back out into the cold, cold snow to track down a really bad man. Bob I did what you asked and picked up one of Mr Mandrake's old coats, not washed or dry-cleaned for some time so the scent should be pretty clear if he's been around recently."

"Right," said Bob, rubbing his hands together in glee, "let's go find ourselves a killer."

As one they all trooped outside and watched as Mr Pickles was introduced to the coat and then let off his leash. At first he sniffed around the Land Rover and then the carport and then he bounded round to the side of the cottage and growled at a briar patch. Bob and Pete prodded it with a stick and came across an old can and several discarded chewing gum wrappers.

"Good grief!" Clara exclaimed, clearly shaken, "I never even knew he was there."

And then Mr Pickles went very still. His nose twitched, his ears flattened and he was off, closely followed by Pete, who was carrying a small hand-held tracking device and much further back by Bob and Brian. Clara and Tavistock took one look at the way they had gone which appeared to be up a vertical slope of scree, scrub and thick gorse and decided to go back in the warm and make a cup of tea.

Chapter 26

Mr Pickles raced and slithered up and then down the slope of the hill overlooking Clara's cottage. He then, after sitting in a small clearing for a few minutes with his nose embedded in a crushed patch of dock and foxgloves, raced off towards a small wooded copse. The copse slunk against the sides of the lowering hill as if it had broken free of the looming plantation of assorted firs and birches marching along the ridge above them.

Just at the apron of the trees Pete could see the outline of a tholtan, a Manx cottage long abandoned by its occupants. Around them silence hung greyly as a weak sun struggled to penetrate the dreary expanse of cloud rolling down from the high hills opposite. Pete was suddenly filled with a kind of dread. The killer had been one step in front of them all the way until now – or had he?

Mr Pickles had disappeared from view and with a clarity born from his covert experience in the Balkans Pete knew without a shadow of a doubt that the place was booby-trapped.

"No!" he screamed as he raced upwards.

Mr Pickles might have been the greediest hound on the planet but he was his greedy hound and …

Bob, who had been struggling to keep up, heard the despairing cry and doubled his efforts as did Brian who although many years younger was actually a little behind him.

Pete crested the rise and dreading that any moment there would be a loud bang followed by bits of his best friend plastering the surrounding countryside, beat his own personal best to the hidden building.

Beside it and hunkered down by a pile of fallen masonry Mr Pickles was happily licking the remains of chocolate and caramel from the foil wrapping of a Tunnocks caramel bar.

"Oh thank God," Pete exclaimed, sinking onto the ground. Mr Pickles looked up and then on seeing the expression on his master's face turned and placing both front paws on Pete's shoulders, leaned in and licked his face.

"Gerroff you great lump," Pete exclaimed. "And don't eat that, it could be poisoned. And I'm not taking you to the vets again for eating foil."

Mr Pickles obediently sat at Pete's feet and gently thumped his large and plumed tail on the ground.

Bob arrived as Pete was carefully checking the perimeter for trip wires.

"What are you doing?" Bob asked.

"Checking for booby traps," came the succinct reply.

"Right," said Bob.

Brian, who had by that time arrived just behind Bob, looked first at Mr Pickles who was now lying on the ground and intently watching his master's every move and then at Pete who was carefully moving a strand of briar with a long stick while lying on his stomach.

"Um ... what exactly is he looking for?" Brian asked, now standing beside his former boss.

"I believe he's looking for a bomb."

"A bomb!" Brian exclaimed. "On the Isle of Man? You

have to be kidding me."

"Nope."

"Shit."

"And a large fan," Bob muttered, taking off his coat and laying it on a fallen log. He then sat on it and extracting a packet of soft mints from his jacket pocket offered one to Brian, who took it almost absentmindedly and sat down next to him.

"You'll get grass stains," Brian advised between chews.

"Old coat." Bob replied, looking out over a vista of scrub, fields and the glen far below them.

"How come you managed to beat me up here." Brian asked mildly impressed.

"Ah well, now that I'm in the private sector I can't afford to pay for someone to do my running for me."

"Ah."

"No fit young police constable eager for the chase."

"What about Pete?"

"A highly paid operative and more importantly ex-SAS. I'd have to pay him at least time and a half."

"Time and a half?"

"Mr Pickles counts as the half."

"Right."

Almost on cue Mr Pickles suddenly growled. It was a long growl with the sort of vibrations that had the hairs on the back of the neck crawling away in horror, while some long-hidden gene on a strand of DNA remembered dark dismal woods with a pair of fangs behind every tree.

Pete shouted, "I think we may have found something," followed by a mumbled curse and the words, "Will you just get off me you daft hound?"

Brian and Bob shot up from their temporary seat and waded through the long grass towards Pete who was lying face down on the ground with Mr Pickles standing on top of him, teeth bared and tail held straight out behind him.

"I presume from the look on Mr Pickles' face that you may indeed have found something," Bob remarked.

"I was just about to enter the premises when the animal knocked me to the ground and now it won't let me up or stop growling, or for that matter drooling."

Bob walked over to the entrance and played a torch around the stones and bramble covering what passed as a doorway. Something above Pete's head glittered just for a moment and Bob edged away very slowly and played his torch on the other side where another glint could clearly be seen between two rough-edged stones.

"Pete," Bob whispered.

"Yes boss."

"I think we may have a problem."

Bob then followed what looked like an almost invisible length of fishing line down the wall along the floor of the entrance and then up the other side.

"Weird," Bob muttered, sitting back on his haunches. "That's really weird."

Pete who was still lying within a millimetre of the stretched line and had now spotted a small black box hidden in the shadow just inside the door sank even further into the ground and moaned.

"Infra-red beam covering the middle of the entrance and a nasty looking package stuck on the other side," he advised Bob who was backing steadily away.

"Pickles lad, how would you like a Mars Bar?" Bob asked, unwrapping the bar of chocolate he always kept in his other pocket. Especially as his wife Moira had him on another diet.

Mr Pickles who momentarily resembled Scooby Doo

spotting a box of Scooby snacks, released his master and trotted over towards Bob. He then sat at Bob's feet, his brown eyes wide and begging.

Pete shuffled backwards on his belly and then when he was sure he was safe stood up and stretched gratefully. Brian, who had been watching, sat on a nearby woody stump and wiped a large handkerchief over his face.

"Oh my God, that was scary," he declared and then on seeing the exchange of amused looks between his three companions including Mr Pickles, added "Please don't tell me that you do this sort of thing all the time."

"No, not all the time," Pete replied. "We normally wait until the weekend."

"Ha bloody ha," Brian moaned and then laughed out loud.

"Pete, that damn dog just winked at me."

"Who – old Pickles?"

"Yes him, the Hound of the Baskervilles, he winked at me. I didn't think that dogs could do that."

"They can't, must have been a nervous tic."

"Tic my arse," Brian snorted as Mr Pickles stared at him.

Bob unwrapped and then dropped the Mars Bar on the ground at Mr Pickles' feet and Mr Pickles devoured it in two slobbering bites.

"So what do we do now?" Pete asked.

"Nothing until Bomb Disposal turn up. I'll give the airport a call and see if anyone is around," Brian replied, reaching into an inner pocket for his mobile.

"Um, hang on half a second," Bob muttered. "I have an idea."

"An idea? Oh no, not one of your 'this is going to not be something I can ever do the paperwork on because they will have me sectioned' kind of ideas, is it?" Brian moaned.

"Possibly," Bob replied with a grin.

"Just tell me," Brian pleaded.

"I think that what we need is someone who can get in and out of small confined spaces without interfering with anything," Bob replied.

Mr Pickles, who had been sniffing around for the slightest crumb of chocolate, sat up and after looking at the doorway and then at Bob slunk swiftly behind his master.

"No not you," Bob declared with a grin. "This is a job for a real pro. Mannanan, don't tell me that you're not here because I'm not completely stupid."

"Really, may I phone a friend?" Mannanan enquired, appearing slowly beside them, as the low cloud that had been moving ever downwards from the southern hills covered the top of the tholtan and then slithered and trailed away in soft wisps at their feet.

"Barty," Mannanan asked, "what have you found?"

"Not sure boss," a disembodied voice replied from the gloomy depths of the derelict building.

"Well there must be something the unsub wanted to hide," Mannanan barked back.

"Unsub?" Brian queried.

"Have you been watching *Criminal Minds* again?" Bob asked, intrigued.

"Tavistock had the box set of series 3 for Christmas and it's somewhat fascinating," Mannanan admitted with a smile.

"Whatever floats your boat," Brian remarked with an equally wide grin.

They waited as the drizzle crept past, coating them in a fine layer of wet which seemed to seep through the seams of their clothing, until finally Barty emerged from the building just as the sun managed to break through the grey above them.

"Can't find anything which may be of help as far as clues

go, apart that is from a homemade explosive device, if that is, bombs look like wads of plasticine wrapped together with parcel tape and have wires going from them to a small battery and a mobile phone."

"Mobile phone?" Bob repeated, a hardening nugget of dread dropping into his mind.

"Yeah, um hate to say this people but um it's just lit up and appears to be receiving an incoming call," Barty shouted at them.

"What!" Pete screamed."Everybody down on the floor now and preferably behind something else."

Mr Pickles, who had up to that point been sniffing at a rabbit hole in hopeful expectation, looked up and then jumped the stone wall surrounding the cottage in a matter of milliseconds; he was joined less than a heartbeat later by Pete, Bob and Brian who had decided that the dog was, at that particular moment in time, the brains of the outfit.

There was a brief flash, followed by a bang and then a steady shower of old rotten wood and blistered stone. Eventually as the noise of falling masonry stopped and Mr Pickles decided it was safe, they all emerged from the sanctuary of their protective wall and found Barty standing in the middle of a stone circle with his arms folded and a decidedly mutinous look on his face. He was in the middle of repeating that he had indeed found nothing and no he had not missed anything when Bob had an idea.

"Barty's right, I reckon Olly didn't leave anything behind except bits of Olly."

"Bits of Olly?" Mannanan asked, turning away from his interrogation of his hapless assistant.

"Yes. I reckon that if we had sent forensics in they would have found something, however small, which would have proved categorically that our missing banker was alive and well. Even if only a smudge of saliva or a rogue fingerprint."

"And so blowing it up ..."

"Means he's still watching us and he's still one step ahead."

***

Later as the evening drew in and Bob sat in front of his TV, his dinner on a tray and a glass of wine beside him on the coffee table he wondered what it was that Oliver Mandrake was so desperate to hide. Desperate enough to kill anyone who knew about it or got in his way.

Chapter 27

Bob was woken at the ungodly hour of seven o'clock by the insistent ringing of a mobile phone.

"It's for you," his long-suffering wife Moira grumbled beside him. "So for God's sake answer it and let me go back to sleep."

Bob groped along the bedside table dislodging a nearly empty glass of water and his reading glasses. The glass hit the floor just as he found his Blackberry and answered it.

"What?" he demanded sleepily, "do you want and this had better be a life and death situation?"

"Just heard from Immigration and our two potential missing victims are here, on the Island."

"Here?" Bob sat up, now wide awake.

"I repeat that they are here on the Island, they both flew in from Manchester and Gatwick yesterday."

"Any idea where and why?" Bob asked.

"No, but I'm almost in the office now and as soon as I can get to a screen and find out I'll let you know," Brian advised before cutting the connection.

Bob shot out of bed, grabbing his dressing gown and raced towards the shower room.

"Where on earth are you going at this hour?" Moira

demanded, sitting bolt upright and glaring at him.

"Out," Bob replied, "and I may be some time."

"Smart arse," Moira muttered, then turned over and went back to sleep.

***

Bob arrived at police headquarters just as Brian was emerging from the building and heading towards his car, keys at the ready.

"Well?" Bob asked, racing to catch him up.

"Both of them are staying at the Sefton and both are over for some small international business jolly, or small country thing. Anyway a local firm of lawyers have organised it together with someone from tourism and several members of the DTI, eager to tell the world that the Island hasn't sunk into recession and is still open for any means of making a bit of filthy lucre. Anyway I've got a car over at the hotel already and both of them are waiting in a private dining room usually used for board meetings. I've given orders that no one goes in or out until I say, and I've got my own assistant tracking down the last name on Clara's list – that should be her now." Brian answered his mobile, listened and barked a gruff, "Thanks, Lil" and switching it off, turned to Bob with a satisfied grin.

"All present and accounted for and it's not even half past eight."

"And it's the 30th September," Bob agreed.

"Exactly," Brian replied, opening his car and motioning for Bob to take the passenger side.

"Let's just hope that Olly doesn't still have something mean and nasty up his sleeve, although for the life of me I can't actually think of what that could be."

***

Tavistock woke to find a cup of steaming coffee sitting on the bedside table and a beaming Richard looming over her clutching the telephone.

"Just off to the office, love," Richard advised, still smiling broadly. "Bob just rang and said not to worry, the last three names are safe and well and helping the police with their enquiries."

Tavistock, sleep suddenly banished, smiled back and reaching up pulled him towards her. "Give us a kiss," she demanded.

Richard happily obliged and then some time later and with a twinkle in his eye set off for the office with a decided spring in his step.

Tavistock waited until she heard the car drive off and took a sip of now cold coffee and sighed with relief. Settling back under the covers she told herself that she would just have a few more zzz's and then she would get up.

It was the sound of something being hauled along the ground that woke her, that and the muffled scream.

Tavistock moaned "Not again" and opened her eyes. The ill-lit sign screwed to the wall in front of her said 'Dutfield's Yard'. Turning her head despite the fact that she had a horrible feeling of certainty as she did so, she saw the two men holding onto a woman struggling between them. There was a flash of silver and just as the knife was raised again voices could be heard coming from behind a low wall to the side of the macabre tableau.

The body was carefully lowered to the ground, blood pumping in a bright and gory stream from the severed artery and then the two men edged quietly away from the wall and out of the yard. They rounded the corner and then ran along a wide main road lit by tall black street lamps spaced at regular intervals. A few yards along a patiently waiting horse and carriage came into view through the smoke-filled gloom.

"Untie the horse and get going Jack," the smarter of the two whispered as he hauled himself into the carriage and shut the door.

"Yes Sir," Jack replied as with shaking hands he untied the horse and clambered up to the driver's seat. It was then that he looked down into Tavistock's eyes and hissed, "Get up here."

Too shocked to answer back, she did as she was told and sat beside him as the horse clattered off along the street. As they neared the end of Whitechapel Road and entered Aldgate there was a hammering from inside the carriage and Jack, cursing under his breath, stopped the carriage. "Get down quickly before he sees, or thinks he sees you," Jack whispered to her.

Tavistock obliged and stood to one side as he jumped down onto the roadside and stepping over the gutter with the reins clutched in his gloved hand, tied the horse to another post.

The cab door opened and the young man got out clutching his black bag.

"Find me another one, and find her quick," he hissed at Jack as he adjusted the folds of his coat and the sleek top hat which shaded his face.

Jack reluctantly headed off down a side street. Tavistock noted the name Mitre Street as she passed the corner and she shuddered as she realised with awful clarity where they were and what was to come.

Figures passed them on the other side of the street and as they hastened along they could see two women deep in conversation against a wall at the entrance to Mitre Square, a third women stood slightly apart smoking on a clay pipe and coughing intermittently.

Tavistock watched as the killer slowed, dug into his pocket

and looked up at the building beside him as if he were looking for something.

"Watcha lookin' for, ducks?" the pipe smoker asked between puffs.

"Um …" the young man looked again at the note in his hand.

"21 Duke Street," he answered, looking around in a nervous fashion.

"Duke Street, eh?" She hawked a glob of saliva onto the pavement in front of her and turned towards her friends.

"Watcha want there?" asked one of the women suspiciously. "Specially a toff like you?"

"Um nothing," he replied, looking embarrassed.

"Looking for a good time are you?" the old crone crowed.

"Um … no. I'm just looking."

They looked up and down the street and then all three of them crossed over and stood around him.

The smell of unwashed rancid flesh and alcohol was almost too much and Tavistock, fighting the urge to be sick, backed away from the partially lit group. Jack, who had been holding a lantern, advanced towards them.

"Oi you lot, leave him alone. He ain't got the money or the time for any services you might have on offer."

"'e said 'e wos just lookin', no harm in that, ducks," one of the three pointed out.

"Look, I'm trying to find an address I got called out to attend a … well, it's a bit embarrassing."

They looked at him and then at the black bag he was carrying and backed off a pace.

"Sorry Doc. Didn't know you was on business," one said apologetically.

"Yeah sorry, Doc," the others chorused.

"Well actually I'm not really a doctor, just training, but I was asked to, as a favour and ..."

"Something go wrong did it?" one of them asked with a knowing look to the others.

"Go wrong?"

"What was it? Some posh friends of yours got a working girl ... ?" the rest of the question hung in the air before them and the young man hung his head looking more than a little bit sheepish.

"Look, it would have caused a lot of embarrassment all round, she was ... is really young and he's married and the mother said that she knew what to do. Look all I want to do is get to 21 Duke Street before I lose the baby, the mother or both."

"Oh well in that case if it's a birth you're attending."

"We thought as it was ..."

"What, what did you think?" The young man asked in a puzzled fashion which appeared to amuse the three women even more.

One of the three stepped in front of him and tapped him on the arm. "Can't have some poor soul dying 'cos of us jawing," she stated, giving her companions a look.

"Duke Street is just a short walk though Mitre Square and then along Church Passage, I'll show you an' your friend how to get there, if you like."

"Thank you, thank you very much," the young man said gratefully, looking deep into her eyes.

She blushed and giggled and then taking his arm and admonishing her friends not to leave without her or take her business she led him across the road and into the square.

They could still hear her friends making ribald comments and promises to wait as they rounded the corner on the right hand side. Away to the left the one solitary street lamp glowed dimly, a pool of light glinting on the cobbled pavement below and on the railings behind it. As they entered the square proper a group of men walked past them. On the opposite side. Jack moved closer to the woman and his master slunk further away into a pool of darkness.

"I never asked your name?" Jack said, watching the men out of the corner of his eye.

"Ooh you 'ave some pretty manners, must 'ave rubbed off from the young gennelman," his companion replied, preening ever so slightly.

"Me name's Catherine, Catherine Eddowes, but you can call me Cat, all me friends do. Even the ones that pay to be friends if you catch my meaning. I could let you 'ave a little treat while your young master is attending to his business, if you have the time and the money."

The men passed by after ensuring that all was well. This was done with a nod from them and a thumbs-up from Catherine.

"I'll think about it," Jack solemnly replied and briefly touched her hand. It was as he turned back towards the direction of Church passage that Tavistock could clearly see the glint of wetness reflected in his eyes as he turned the lamp up.

"It's a good thing you've got that lamp," the women remarked. "It's as black as the gates of hell on this side o' the square."

"I suppose you know this area well?" her companion remarked.

"Oh yeah. That shop on the corner what we passed is a tailors and then next to it is an old house."

"Looks dark and well ... haunted."

"Abandoned, that's what it is. Locked up and empty. Crying shame when you think of how many round 'ere is desperate for a room for the night. Just like that one opposite – bleedin' absentee landlords."

"The one beyond the railings?"

"Yeah, next to the constable's."

"Constable?" Jack and his master exchanged a glance.

"Oh 'e's not there, won't be till morning, works the night shift, see, 'e don't bother with us."

It was as they were passing a long wooden fence on their right that Jack stumbled and the lamp went out.

"Ere watchit!" she exclaimed, and then just as she was about to scream a hand covered her mouth and the knife sliced into her clothing. She struggled and was half-pulled, half-dragged into the dark corner between the beginning of the fence and the abandoned building that she had previously pointed out.

The knife slashed out again and she managed to turn her head and kicked out. The knife sliced against the side of her face nicking an ear and she screamed afresh. The sound was muffled by a heavy coat, which had been thrown over her head by Jack.

"For pity's sake cut her throat now, before they hear and come running," Jack hissed, terrified.

"Coward. I was looking forward to playing with her."

"We don't have time for that, not with those hags waiting around the corner for her to come back, and I bet they know to the minute how long it will take to get back from Duke Street," Jack hissed, holding onto his coat and the struggling woman.

"Oh very well," his companion sulkily replied and then with alarming speed thrust the knife up to the hilt into her chest, in the ravaged area between her breasts and then as Jack removed the coat from her face, neatly severed the artery in her neck. Catherine Eddowes sunk onto the pavement and Jack went and stood against the fence, trembling. Tavistock stood beside him and tried desperately to not hear the sounds made as the killer in front of them went about his gory pleasure. Finally sated he stood up clutching her bloody apron and without looking at them hurried off towards the dark maw of Church Passage.

"Jack – hurry up," he hissed as he raced away.

Jack was about to follow when he stopped, and grabbing Tavistock's shoulders he looked deep into her eyes and whispered, "Look around, remember all this, remember where we are. Don't let it happen again."

Tavistock stared back and then nodded.

He smiled then, a smile of deep warmth and released her.

"His father told me to look after him, whatever he did. And I have … just not any more. He says that they have no meaning, no worth, no value … but she was Cat to her friends."

He sighed and then as he turned away and faded into the dark Tavistock could still hear his voice urging her to remember where she was.

Chapter 28

"Arghh!" she screamed and sat bolt upright finding with almost as great a shock as with relief that she was in her own bed, in her own room, in her own century.

"Oh God help me," she murmured, trying to drive the awful visions out of her head.

"Tavistock, Tavistock, look at me."

Tavistock opened her streaming eyes and looked straight into the concerned deep brown orbs of Mannanan Mac Lir.

"I don't understand," she cried, tears streaming down her face. "I just don't understand what he wants."

"Who?" Mannanan asked. "Who don't you understand?"

"The man who helped Jack the Ripper, the man the Ripper calls Jack."

Mannanan looked at her, a strange twisted half-smile played around his mouth and then with a sigh he moved towards the window and looked out at the fresh bright new morning.

"I think that you had better get dressed and find out," Mannanan replied. "Don't you?"

***

Later that day she and Bob sat nursing coffees in Coffee Republic and watched the passers-by with something approaching complete disinterest.

"So Brian says it's all over, bar the shouting and the singing of the fat lady," Bob remarked.

"I guess so."

"You don't look convinced."

"That's because I'm not."

"Why?"

"Because it's too easy."

"Right."

"And because Oliver Mandrake is still out there."

"Well, I can't see what he can do. We have the names on the list or at least the ones still left alive and ..."

Tavistock felt something pass through her and shuddered.

"What?"

"Something walked over my grave. You said you have a list."

"Clara's list."

"But what if Clara's list isn't Oliver's list?"

"I'm not following."

"I'm not sure I do either but bear with me on the grounds that I'm a writer and therefore have a fiendishly clever brain that not only thinks outside the envelope but the post-box as well."

"Okay."

"I mean it Bob, I ..." Tavistock frowned in concentration and then began to think aloud.

"If I was writing this out as a plotline, I would want, as well as bodies, a clear and logical motive."

"Following you so far."

"Good."

"And admittedly the motive for bumping off the first three

victims, and I'm including the poor old accountant, is because they knew how Oliver had been fiddling the accounts of companies he had taken over and basically asset-stripped. Even though they were clearly viable before he offered them the gift of fiscal recovery."

"Right."

"Thing is, from what you've said, via the lips of Brian, the other people on Clara's list only know what we already know so …"

"So?"

"Why would he want to bump them off as well? Seems like a complete waste of time and also a bit stupid and from what we know Oliver Mandrake is anything but that."

"True, oh wise one."

"Cut it out, I'm serious."

"Okay, so what do you suggest?"

"Well in the time honoured way of the master of fiction and crime in particular, dear old Agatha, we have three main motives for killing. Love … and I don't see that as a motive in this particular case."

"Nor do I, oh great one, so carry on."

"Character weakness, i.e. there is no other option unless you want to be held accountable for something."

"Don't think, having met the nasty little creep, that weakness is one of his traits."

"Nor do I."

"So what's the third option?"

"Greed, or money. Agatha always followed the money. It's like fraud, you follow the money all the way to the top."

"And we know he's a sociopath."

"A nice name for the average axe-carrying psycho," Tavistock ruefully agreed.

"Doesn't get us any closer to finding him though."

"You know before I came here, I had a really weird and horrible dream."

"Oh yes?"

"And I asked our mutual friend Mannanan how come he couldn't just track Oliver Mandrake down, making things a lot easier all round, and he said that he could only track down those with a soul since he had forfeited his minor deity rights and that it was his considered opinion that young Oliver had already sold his soul to the opposition, as it were."

"Passed over to the dark side at an early age, either that or the little sod never had one to start with."

"The early Celts would certainly agree with that." Tavistock paused and absentmindedly added more sugar to her cooling mug. "Speaking of which, our old Celtic friend did say that he was sure that Oliver was still on the Island, which rather begs the question why?"

"Why indeed. And young Brian may have the answer."

At that moment Brian Clague had come in off the street and headed to the counter picking up a large chocolate muffin on the way.

After a minute or so he joined them clutching the muffin, a steaming mug of coffee and a wad of papers.

"Why so solemn?" he asked, joining them.

"Tavistock here says our mutual invisible friend reckons Oliver Mandrake is still here and we are both wondering why. She's also pointed out in her tricksy little way that Clara's list may not be Oliver's."

"A conclusion I have also been gently coming around to," Brian muttered, reluctantly handing the wad of papers over.

"Why is that?" Bob asked, glancing through the sheets of neatly typed lists and statements.

"Mr Mandrake has definitely not left the Island and our three potential victims know even less than we do about him." Brian bit into his muffin and frowned before continuing, "The only thing I do know is that after talking at length to both his assistant, his line manager and his wife, Oliver Mandrake was going to attend all the little jollies that our almost victims were."

"Jollies?"

"A tour around the Island to see the Lady Isabella, Milntown where they were all going to have a grand lunch."

"Lucky sods," Tavistock muttered, hungrily eyeing up the remains of Brian's cake.

"They would then have a wonderful ride on the electric tram back to Douglas and their hotel. Later to be picked up and carted off to Peel for a ghost walk along the wynds and passageways. After which they get to have a hog roast at Peel Castle complete with jugglers, pipers and traditional dancing.

"Ghost walk," Tavistock breathed and then desperately tried to catch hold of the thought fleetingly waving a large flag around in her head.

"What?" Brian asked.

"Nothing, it's gone."

"If it's important it will be back," Bob advised sagely

"I wouldn't bet on it." she replied.

***

Later that evening as she stirred in the coconut milk while preparing a supper of Thai chicken and sticky rice, the elusive thought which had now managed to get a front row seat, waved a blazing torch around and bounced up and down in desperation.

"Ghost walk!" she cursed. She'd been on it recently with a few friends as a bit of a laugh and there had been a place, a hidden square with a wooden fence on one side and two passageways leading off at the end, just like in Mitre Square.

"Remember this," Jack had urged.

"Shit, shit and double shit!" she cursed, switching off the gas under both burners.

"He didn't mean the murder, he meant the *place*."

She dropped the wooden spoon and raced to the telephone.

"Brian!" she screamed after he had eventually answered his mobile phone. "The ghost walk – he's going to kill the next two during the ghost walk."

Brian greeted her words with a deathly silence.

"Brian."

"Are you sure about this?"

"I'm sure. I'm really, really sure."

"Then put your coat on and I'll pick you up in fifteen minutes, and let's just hope we aren't too late."

Chapter 29

Jenna Parish ticked the names off her list as they exited the coach in ones and twos and giggling, rather inebriated, threes and fours. The Chinese contingent, who had pointedly ignored their Japanese counterparts who were gaily taking photographs of anything that moved, edged slowly from the bus and then stood next to her.

"And this ghost walk is part of your heritage?" asked Mr Hanong who had arrived that day from Shanghai via Manchester.

Jenna looked up from her list and with her usual fixed and sunny smile nodded.

"Oh yes. It's part of our culture although our guide who is a very learned historian will be better placed to help you answer any questions," she replied, ticking the penultimate name.

"Then we will ensure that we are right at the front," Mr Hanong smiled back at her.

Jenna watched them move away towards a man dressed in a top hat and Victorian greatcoat and wished that she had a large warm coat too, as it was getting really cold and all she had was a smart but thin silk business suit.

The last passenger alighted and was ticked off her list and

then she listened as the organiser of the trip introduced their guide and explained what would happen. Their guide, a man she had vaguely met at some dinner and also seen perform at the Peel Centenary Centre and the Gaiety Theatre, took over to a round of applause and introduced himself, warning them not to get lost or lag behind in case the black dog was about, or even worse, he added as an afterthought. Silence greeted this remark as all the guests, even some of the Manx ones looked around uncertainly.

A sea fog had been creeping inshore and now it sat in a sullen fashion along the promenade as if awaiting its cue to crawl further into the town itself.

Jenna shivered, remembering a ghost story she had once read about a ghost walk which had gone badly wrong and wondered if the driver had anything warm she could borrow, and then realising that her charges were off the starting blocks and quickly disappearing up a cobbled lane, hurried after them cursing silently in her head.

"I'm not a bloody sheepdog," she thought miserably as she hurried to catch them up.

She had almost reached the group now standing on the opposite side of the road and looking up at an old doorway, when a hand came out of the shadows and grabbed her, pulling her back out of view of her charges.

She spun around and gasped in shock and then as she saw who it was, a certain amount of delight.

"Olly."

"Hi, Jenna love."

"What are you doing here?"

And then she remembered what the police had said and more importantly what they hadn't but the rumour mill had and backed away.

"The police?" she asked hesitantly. "They told us to get in

touch if we saw you. They said you were ..."

"I know, I know, all a dreadful mistake and one that I'm about to put right, a little theatrically of course but it will all be okay on the night as they say." Olly laughed brightly and smiled down at her, radiating warmth and humour.

"Really?" she breathed, looking into intense blue eyes which twinkled gaily back at her. She had always had a soft spot for OllyMandrake especially after the last staff party where they had ended up back in his hotel room.

"Oh yes. I know exactly who has it in for me and I've got a nasty little surprise waiting for them. But first ..." he whispered, kissing the nape of her neck as he moved closer, "I want you to do something for me."

"Anything," she breathed, as a cold shiver went down her spine.

"Put this on."

Opening her eyes, she looked at the Victorian dress he was holding and screwed up her nose.

"What, that old thing?"

"Yes this old thing, perfectly serviceable and yes I know it's not your colour but it's probably a lot warmer than what you have on."

Jenna grinned ruefully.

"How did you know?"

"Because I know you little Jenna, and you like to be snug and warm."

Jenna giggled coquettishly and took off her jacket.

"Now the shirt," Oliver ordered.

"But can't I just throw it over the top?" she asked.

"No, you'll spoil the lines."

"But someone may see."

"Who? The invisible man? Darling Jen there are shops on either side and an office in front which is closed, the only one here is me and I really don't mind at all," Oliver grinned back and winked at her.

"Oh very well," she grumbled, unbuttoning her blouse. "But if it gets ruined, this blouse cost a fortune in Harvey Nicks."

"I'll get it dry cleaned or buy you another," Oliver promised. "Only do hurry or we will miss the finale."

Jenna removed her blouse and Oliver carefully helped her into the dress and did up the zip at the back. Critically he turned her around and then produced a scarf from his pocket and tied it around her head.

"There you go, even your own mother wouldn't recognise you."

Jenna walked over to the office window and surveyed her reflection.

"Good, because I look like a Victorian prossie," she exclaimed disdainfully. "Really poor and common especially with this thing over my head."

"Lady of negotiable affection," Oliver laughed and then leant down and kissed her on the mouth. "And you look lovely," he added. "Now come on, get your skates on or we won't be there in time for the surprise."

***

Mr Hanong listened with ever increasing fascination to the guide as they wound their way around the small cramped passageways and threaded between the quaint stone mews filled with tubs of brightly coloured flowers, which glistened under the intermittent street lamps. After they had climbed a little way up some steps they emerged into a small square surfaced in tarmac and edged with old buildings and a low wooden fence. At the far end a couple stood dressed in Victorian costume. For some reason that he couldn't remember he suddenly thought of his visit to Whitechapel the previous year and a walking tour he and his wife and children had done there.

"It is like the Jack Ripper," he murmured to his wife in a low voice.

The guide, who had also noticed the couple, frowned; he was sure that no one was supposed to be here, the next tableau wasn't due until they reached the old ruined church at the top of the hill.

He was just about to ask them what was going on when the woman suddenly screamed and started to struggle. There was a flash of silver and then a knife was plunged into her stomach. Mr Hanong was very impressed as were the others in the tour.

"Oh well done," said one, "it looks almost real."

The knife was pulled out and the woman screamed again as the knife was raised and her throat was pulled back by her assailant.

"Look, I can see the blood and it looks awfully realistic," A woman pointed out as the Japanese group took yet even more photographs with their mobile phones.

"That's because it bloody well is!" Bob bellowed racing past them closely followed by Brian and two police constables.

"Oliver Mandrake – I arrest you for the murders …" Brian shouted at him.

Oliver looked at his pursuers and almost threw the writhing, screaming form of Jenna at them before disappearing down a side alley.

They found his cloak and hat at the entrance and then there was nothing but a slowly rising mist creeping softly and silently along the passageway.

"Right!" Brian bellowed, "I want the whole area sealed off. Inspect every nook and cranny and wake up every single person in this road and the surrounding area he's not a ghost he's a man and he must be hiding somewhere."

Tavistock who had run towards the stricken girl, knelt down and then at the look of terror on the girl's face held her in her arms until the ambulance arrived and the paramedics took over.

"Please, I have to tell you something, it's important," Jenna sobbed as her body was wracked in spasms of pain.

"I'm listening," Tavistock replied, as she applied pressure to the jagged wound in a desperate attempt to stem the flow.

"A week ago Oliver bought a place in the Canaries, he said it was a surprise for his wife. But that I wasn't to tell anyone. Only I knew about it and he transferred the funds to the account himself."

She whimpered as another shaft of unspeakable pain wanted to make her die then and there but held it in.

"But this is the important bit. I went into work this morning really early before I had to collect the visitors and it wasn't there. The details weren't there."

"Can you remember the address?"

"I think so. I wasn't paying much attention thing is it wasn't in his name it was in …"

"It was in whose name?" Tavistock urged.

"It …" and then Jenna closed her eyes and faded into that black unfeeling night.

Tavistock grimly gripped her hand and whispered, "Hold on child, hold on, you just live – don't let the bugger win."

Later as she watched the ambulance door close and saw it screaming off into the night, blue lights blazing and sirens blaring she looked down at the blood on her hands and swore vengeance.

Chapter 30

Clara heard the knock on the door and debated whether or not to answer it; her dogs stirred in front of the fire and then went back to sleep.

The knock turned into hammering and a voice shouted through the keyhole,

"Clara, if you don't open this open this door right here and now I'm going to climb up onto the roof and tip petrol down your chimney."

Clara gave a heavy sigh, abandoned the crossword she was trying to solve, got up out of her chair, crossed the room and opened the door.

"Tavistock," she muttered crossly and then on seeing her face as she half-stumbled inside changed her tone to one of concern.

"Tavistock my dear, what on earth has happened? Sit down, sit here in front of the fire, no don't move. I'll get you a drink. Sherry all right? Haven't been to the shops for a few days and there's nothing else in that's drinkable."

Tavistock nodded as she studied the flames in front of her, the soot behind sparkling red as the heat burnt it away.

"I've got Croft Original or Harveys Bristol Cream?

"Croft," Tavistock answered, her mouth on auto pilot as

her body began to shut down.

Clara went to a small sideboard, extracted a bottle from a side cupboard together with two sherry glasses and after filling both to the brim handed one to Tavistock. Sitting back in her chair she placed hers on the small round table on which she'd left a half-drunk mug of coffee and her reading glasses.

Tavistock took a gulp of her drink and after letting the warmth slide down her throat exclaimed, "Oh God but I needed that."

Clara sat back in her chair and picking up her glass took a sip as Tavistock turned her face towards her, it was then that Clara realised that she had been crying.

Suddenly concerned, she leant forward and patted her friend's hand.

"So tell me," she murmured as softly as she could. "Tell me everything."

"That bastard Oliver Mandrake attempted to kill his assistant Jenna tonight. He got her to dress up in Victorian costume and re-enactedthe part of Catherine Eddowes. She's going to live because Jack the Ripper's assistant, driver, friend, butler – whatever you like to call him – told me to remember the scene and I did."

"There has been another murder?" Clara exclaimed.

"Nearly two more tonight. As well as attempting to kill Jenna he'd tried to cut the throat of one of the actors who play various parts during the Peel Ghost Walk."

"Tried?"

"Fortunately for that particular man he was wearing a neck brace under his costume, apparently he had some sort of neck injury from working on computers compounded by whiplash from a car crash some months ago."

"Lucky for him."

"Yes, although Oliver did knock him out as they struggled

and he may have a fractured skull. We came across him groggily wandering around outside the house they change and keep the costumes in."

"And the girl, Jenna?"

"Lost a lot of blood and is in ICU, they think that she will live. I hope she does."

"Tavistock, this isn't your fault."

"No?"

"No," Clara declared emphatically and then she reached over and clasped Tavistock's hand in hers. "If anything *I* brought Oliver here. If I hadn't started investigating Thomas's death none of this would have happened."

"Actually Clara, I rather think it would."

"How so?"

"Because Oliver is working from his list not yours. Your snooping was just an added bonus."

They sat in silence. A silence broken only by the steady ticking of a solitary wall clock and the gently crackling fire of greenwood logs.

"Thing is, I can't understand why he chose to copy the Ripper, unless ..." Tavistock suddenly remembered the signing and the young suits at the back. Desperately she tried to run the session through in her head, that moment when she had looked around to gauge the audience to try and tailor her talk to fit them. There had been another man in a suit behind a pillar at the back and later he had asked a question, after she had done the signing and had held an impromptu Q&A in the coffee shop upstairs.

"There was a man at one of my signings, before all this happened and he asked me why I thought the Ripper started and I told him that maybe he'd seen a play or something that had set him off. Clara, he asked me which one and I said *The Strange Case of Doctor Jekyll and Mr Hyde*."

"Why did you say that?" Clara asked.

"I have no idea, it just popped into my head. How odd, it was before the dream."

"What dream?"

"The dream I had of the Ripper and his servant Jack going to the theatre. There was a girl, a girl in the shadows. I think she was important but I have no idea why. And …"

"And?"

"And this seems strange but I woke up singing 'Anyone here seen Kelly, Kelly from the Isle of Man'."

Tavistock stopped as her friend's face drained of all colour.

"You think that Oliver Mandrake was there and decided to kill in the footsteps of the Ripper?"

"Yes. Yes, thinking about it now, yes. Yes I do. Clara, what's the matter?"

"Do you have the knife?"

"The knife?Tavistock queried.

"Yes. The knife, the one that you said you had bought in London."

"It's in the car. I locked it in the glove compartment. I thought it would stop me having bad dreams."

"And did it?"

"No."

"Tavistock, listen to me. Go and get the knife, go and get it now and bring it here."

Tavistock nodded and did as she was bid. Clara waited until she had gone and then went upstairs to her bedroom. She crossed the room to the small chest at the end of her bed and extracted the old box from its cluttered depths. She then took it back downstairs and laid it carefully on the table beside her chair. Tavistock arrived back ten minutes later with the knife still in its plastic bag and made to hand it to Clara who backed away and said, "No. Just hold it on your lap while I get something for you to put it on."

A small low table by the window was moved over to sit between their respective fireside chairs and Tavistock carefully lay the knife on the tables gnarled and oddly stained surface.

Clara looked at it and then at Tavistock.

"This is the Ripper's knife," she stated.

"I think so, yes," Tavistock admitted.

"And you are now so linked to it that you can see things and it's not even in your hands, just nearby."

Tavistock swallowed and looked again at the weapon lying innocently in the ruddy glow of the fire.

"Yes."

"Good."

Tavistock looked up at her in surprise but before she could say anything Clara continued blithely on. "Now listen to me. I called Bob and a well friend of mine while you were out and they should be here soon. We have to stop Oliver from killing his final victim. If you're right, and I think you are, Oliver is not killing to my agenda but his and for some reason he picked the Ripper's killings. What we really need to know is why. Understood?"

"Yes."

"And now we wait."

They sipped their sherry in silence and then Clara got up and poured them out another glass which they had almost finished before there was another knock on the door. It was Bob, smothered in wool against the chill of the unseasonably cold and frosty night.

As he sat down on a chair hastily pulled away from the window, Mannanan and Barty appeared silently beside him.

"What the –" Tavistock exclaimed as Clara and Mannanan

exchanged equally worried looks.

Mannanan cleared his throat and Barty went and stood quietly behind him.

"Tavistock, Bob and Clara join hands, and Tavistock don't ask any questions as we simply don't have the time."

They did as they were told and then Mannanan shimmied through them and carefully taking the knife from the table, placed it in Tavistock's lap.

"Tavistock, let go of Bob and Clara." Mannanan ordered. "Bob, Clara, hold onto her elbows and unclasp from each other and hold one of my hands instead. Good, now we have a circle. Tavistock, open the bag and hold the knife."

"But –"

"We need to find Kelly," Mannanan stated sadly. "The girl I couldn't help. Kelly from the Isle of Man."

Tavistock opened the bag, removed the knife and held it in both hands. The long silver blade caught the firelight and burned red and then the walls of the cottage disappeared, to be replaced with the grime and soot-blackened walls of a tall tenement house. In front of one of the doors leading onto the road a tall greatcoated figure pleaded with someone inside.

"Nan, just let me in. Nan, I can explain, I can sort it out, answer every question. Please Nan, just let me in."

The door opened and he was let inside. They all followed almost as if he was dragging them in his wake. Together they moved from an ill-lit hallway into a small sparse room on the ground floor. It contained a single bed and a table set with a few tea things, a chair neatly arranged beside it. The only other item of furniture was a wardrobe, its door partly open revealing its meagre contents and a nurse's cape and cap hung limply from the handle as if the occupant had been disturbed while either putting them on or taking them off.

The woman backed away from the young man and stood

by the window.

"Nan, look you know that I love you."

"You say that now."

"But I do."

"I burnt the clothes just like you asked me to. I took them to the boiler room. They weren't old and there were bloodstains."

"Just old stains, too stained to wear. You know me Nan, I'm just a dandy at heart."

"They were bloodstains, fresh blood and you know it as well as I do," she replied, holding onto the back of the chair as if willing it to give her strength.

"Nan, Nan, my beautiful Nan. They were just old hunting clothes, I hadn't realised how bad they had got and they smelt."

"Then why didn't you just throw them away?"

"What, and be accused of something horrible?"

"Like being the Ripper?" she asked, her expression earnest in the light from the single oil lamp on the table.

"Now who's being fanciful?" he replied, making a move towards her.

"Don't touch me, just don't," she urged, a tear spilling from her eye.

"Look, I don't know why you're so upset, I really don't but …"

"Uncle John told me," she suddenly exclaimed.

"Uncle John? Uncle John told you what?"

"Well he's not really an uncle, more like a second or third cousin but …"

"Yes, I get it, he's some sort of distant relation, so what?"

"He's kind and he helps me out."

"I bet he does," the young man sniggered.

"Don't be so insulting," she shouted at him. "He's a kind and honest man which is more than can be said for you."

"Kind and honest, Nan? Now I am hurt. Haven't I always been kind to you? And as for support, haven't I always left a little something towards expenses? Well, haven't I? And you know how little I have left over from my allowance."

"Not as little as from a nurse's wage," she replied with feeling.

"Look, I didn't come here to quarrel."

"Then what have you come for?"

"I want to know why you ran from the ward when you saw me."

"Uncle John said that you were engaged to be married. He said you were using me, he said that you didn't love me, that you never had."

"Damn this uncle of yours," he shouted while privately vowing that if he ever met him he'd ensure that the wonderful Uncle John didn't live to tell another tale about him.

"Now listen to me Nan, my own sweet little Nan. Yes, I'm engaged, I have been for a while but I don't love her, not like I love you. The only reason I'm marrying at all is to secure her lands. Her father's estate is next to mine and she has the mills from her mother's family. It's just business Nan, that's all, just business."

"And what about me?" she asked, her voice breaking on a sob.

"You will always be my beloved Nan and even though I can't give you my hand, I can give you my heart."

She stopped crying and with a sigh launched herself at his chest. He struggled out of his coat, dropping it on the floor and half-carried, half-pulled her to the bed.

She lay back on the pillows and closed her eyes and as she did he kissed her while at the same time he reached into the pocket of his loose jacket and plunged the knife that he now held deep into her chest. She screamed, the sound bubbling up as blood began to fill her lungs.

"I'm sorry Nan my love, but you will eventually tell someone about the clothes and that someone will tell someone else. If it's any consolation though I really do love you. Enough to make it a clean kill."

He watched as the light in her eyes faded and then he pulled the knife out and slit her throat, bearing down so hard on the blade that the neck was severed down to her spine. He got up then and slit her dress, and then he spotted the window, the curtains of which were half-closed. He got up, closed them fully and moving the lamp nearer, proceeded to open up the abdomen and one by one he removed the organs which he spread across the bloodied coverlet, and then the heart.

The heart though was carefully placed into the black bag and then without warning he seemed to completely lose his temper.

"And don't look at me!" he hissed. The knife flashed in his hand as he hacked away at her face until suddenly spent, he seemed to come to his senses.

Hastily he picked up his bag, thrust the knife inside, shrugged himself into his coat and hearing a noise in the hallway looked around desperately for a way out. Silently he padded over to the window and extinguishing the lamp opened it and carefully climbed over the sill and disappeared into the night beyond.

Pushing his way through the crowd on the way to his lodgings he didn't notice a man muffled to the eyes in a long scarf and bowler hat who stared after him.

The gloom and dirt, sights and smells of a Victorian London night faded with the last sound of wheels on cobbles and Tavistock, Bob, Clara and Mannanan found themselves once again in Clara's warm and now very snug front room.

Tavistock dropped the knife and sank backwards into her chair.

"Anybody want a drink, because after that I sure as hell want to down at least a bottle or two," Clara declared, going to the cabinet.

"Yes," they all emphatically replied as she shakily poured out three very full glasses of sherry.

Bob looked at his for a brief moment and then tipped his head back and downed it in one.

"More," he demanded, handing Clara back the glass.

Chapter 31

Later as they sat in shocked and contemplative silence Bob asked the room in general, "So the last person he murdered was the one he said he loved?"

"Apparently so," Tavistock agreed.

"Fine way of showing it," Bob muttered, looking into the dregs of his sherry glass.

"He was a typical sociopath. I doubt if they can ever truly love anyone other than themselves," Clara declared as she got up and fetched the nearly empty sherry bottle. Pouring them each a last small amount she added, "And when this is gone we will have to consume the sweet and sticky stuff. Unless the local off licence delivers."

Tavistock looked at her and then wondered aloud if anybody delivered.

"Don't know," Clara replied. "I'll check the A–Z."

"A-Z." Tavistock repeated, a little the worse for wear, and then sat bolt upright as a horrible and nasty thought had hit her.

"What if, what if … no, it couldn't be that simple."

"What couldn't?" Bob and Clara asked in unison.

"What if you wanted to hide something? Wanted to hide it in plain sight."

"You'd hide it with a lot of things nearly or entirely the same," Clara replied thoughtfully.

"Exactly. Like Christie's *The A, B, C Murders*. You hide a murder in amongst a lot of others."

"Oliver Mandrake has the complete Agatha Christie collection," Bob advised them, sitting bolt upright. "So perhaps …"

"The only killing that never made sense to me was Kelly's, so what if that was the only one the Ripper actually needed to do," Tavistock mused, her eyes glowing with excitement.

"The others were all red herrings."

"Exactly."

"He killed Mary Jane Kelly because she was in the way, not because she thought he was the Ripper," Bob breathed.

"But he loved her," Clara declared.

"Said he loved her."

"And if Oliver is doing the same thing then the last victim will be the one he says he loves."

"Well in that case it would be Fion, his wife," Bob barked before adding, "and I bet he won't wait until 9th November to do it. I bet the little sod is right now trying to get inside his own house."

Galvanised, he extracted his mobile from his pocket and finding a place in the corner of the lounge where he could get satellite coverage phoned Clive.

"Clive, no don't say anything, just listen. Oliver Mandrake is on his way home. Do we have anything at all that isn't being covered?"

"I'll check."

They all waited in a suspenseful silence which was finally broken by Clive.

"Nothing … Oh, hang on, one of the sensors near the garage, one of the extra ones we installed yesterday has gone off."

"Is Pete around?"

"He should be at home by now, feeding that hound of his and watching something stupid on the box."

"Well give him a bell and tell him to get down there. I'll ring Brian and tell him Oliver is on his way and he's mad, dangerous and more than likely armed with more than a boning knife this time round."

Tavistock and Clara exchanged identical horrified looks and Tavistock reached for the Harveys.

Bob disconnected and then punched in a new number and waited for someone to answer. He waited and waited, growing more worried and impatient with every second. He was almost about to disconnect when it was answered.

"Bob?" a worried voice could be heard to ask.

"Fion love, don't ask questions. Olly is on his way and he's armed and dangerous. Where are the kids?"

"At a friend's. And I know about Olly, he rang and said he was being framed, he said that he had to get away and he needed me to sign a few things first."

"Don't sign anything and don't let him in."

"But he has a key."

"Pete and I changed all the locks when you were out yesterday and slipped the new key into your bag when you returned."

"Oh."

"I want you to find somewhere with a lock, preferably a strong somewhere and barricade yourself in. Pete is on his way and so are the police but whatever you do, do not go anywhere near your husband. Fion, you must promise me this. You do not go anywhere near him."

"I promise," she muttered.

"Good girl," Bob replied before disconnecting.

"Yes, good girl," Oliver Mandrake repeated with a smile as

he took the mobile phone away from her mouth and placed it on the bedside table.

Chapter 32

Bob sat back and placed the mobile on the table.

"Well that's all right then," Clara remarked cheerily. "So who wants another little drinkie?"

Bob looked up at that and met her eyes and the look on his face was one of horror.

"What! What is it?" she asked. "Come on Bob, you're scaring me and the Harveys wasn't that bad – a bit on the sweet side I grant you but ..."

"It's too late," he cried, sinking back into his armchair, a look of profound despair replacing his earlier horrified expression.

Tavistock turned towards him. "What's too late?"

"Oliver Mandrake is already there."

"There?"

"In the house with Fion and probably in the same room."

They all stared at him with their mouths open; even Mannanan was momentarily shocked into immobility.

"How the hell can you possibly know that?" Tavistock almost shouted at him, willing him to be mistaken.

"Fion saw us change the locks she was there, and we had a code word to use if she was in trouble, that word was 'promise'."

"Oh my God you asked her to promise and she …"

"Said that she would 'promise'. He's there and he probably has a weapon of some sort and it's at least half an hour by car and even if we could fly it would take at least ten minutes."

Clara covered her mouth, the vision of Mary Kelly's last moments echoing in her mind's eye. "I'm going to be sick," she mumbled and fled the room.

"Do something. Please can't you do something, anything at all, give her some time?" Tavistock pleaded as she fixed Mannanan with a desperate look.

"What do you suggest?"

"Anything, throw stuff around, grab the knife, stop the bullet, anything!"

Mannanan and Barty exchanged looks and then vanished. The words, "I'll try," hung in the air as they vanished.

***

Oliver sat astride his terrified wife and raised the shimmering knife above his head.

"It's all right my love. I won't do it exactly à la Ripper, I'll cut your heart out after you're dead, I promise."

"You complete and utter bastard," Fion hissed. "Did you actually ever love me?"

"Oh yes, in my own way. But then I really don't love anyone as much as me and you, my lovely wife, know far more about me than is good for you."

"Like what?" she snarled. "The colour of your favourite shirt, or the fact that you can't switch on a computer without taking a punt on something? Or that you'll screw anything pretty in a skirt with a pulse?"

"You knew about that?"

"Oh yes, I knew all about the Jennas and the Izobelles," Fion replied bitterly.

"That must have hurt."

Something passed across her face, some emotion.

"It didn't matter, they were your playthings, recreational if you like. Besides I had you, you and the children. For pity's sake Olly, what will they do with both parents gone?"

"Ah yes, the children."

Fion looked up at him and realised that he wasn't even affected by the thought of his own children suffering; instead his face had hardened into a cruel mask of the man she had thought that she had known.

"You can't possibly be jealous? Not of your own kids?" she thought aloud as the truth became clear.

"You wanted the little brats not me," he hissed.

"I still don't know why. I mean look what they did to you." He punched her in the stomach and she winced, too shocked to reply.

"You used to be so firm, firm all over. I loved that slim girlish body of yours and now all you have are breasts and stretch marks."

"Oh grow up, you total and utter little shit," she snarled, spitting in his face.

He wiped it away and smiled back down at her.

"You know I've always liked it when you've fought back."

Fion lay horrified as he hardened and screamed as he pushed her nightdress up above her hips.

"No," she screamed. "Oh God no!"

"Why not? You're still my wife and I paid for all of this." He waved the knife around and then held it to her throat, pushing down hard enough to break the skin.

"Just think, your final memories of this world will be sex with me."

"No!" Fion screamed again and despite the pain tried to struggle out of his grip.

He laughed and then as he was pulling down his trousers with one hand while still trapping his wife with the weight of his much larger body, cutting into her neck with the knife he held in the other hand he heard a voice behind him calmly state, "The lady said no."

"And who's going to stop me little man, you?" And Oliver Mandrake laughed out loud.

"No, not me, him," the voice replied.

And then Oliver heard the growl. The type of low growl which resonated far into his bones. A primeval memory raised itself and for the first time in his life he was utterly terrified.

And then he felt the soft breath at the back of his neck. Razor sharp teeth bit into the hand holding the knife and sunk into flesh and bone. He screamed as a tendon snapped and Fion, finding the pressure on top of her slacken, wriggled sideways and flung herself from the bed, leaving her husband looking into the stone-cold eyes of Mr Pickles.

"Get this fucking animal off me," he screamed, terrified as Mr Pickles glared back at him.

Pete then pushed the barrel of the gun he had been carrying against the back of Oliver's head and whispered, "I can tell him to let go but I don't trust you not to try something. So before I give him the word I just want you to know that I'm ex-SAS, I've killed for Queen and country and now I kill for money. So don't for one minute think that I won't blow your brains out from the back of your head, because I will."

Oliver muttered something and Pete leant over him. "I didn't quite hear that."

"I promise not to do anything, anything at all. Just get it off me."

"Mr Pickles, release," Pete ordered and Mr Pickles reluctantly let go of the almost death-like grip he had on Oliver Mandrake and slunk backwards off the bed.

"The police will be here in a minute or two," Pete advised and then added, "So Fion would you like to throw something warmer on and let them in?"

Fion gratefully grabbed her dressing gown from the floor where it had fallen and rushed from the room. Oliver lay face down on the bed and tried to think as Mr Pickles sat glaring at him.

Pete removed the gun from the back of Oliver's neck and took a careful step backwards while still covering him with his weapon.

"Mr Pickles," he ordered. "If he moves other than to breathe you can kill him."

Mr Pickles almost smiled, his whole stance looked eager to please. Kill also meant eat and he knew in every straining sense that the creature on the bed still had a Mars Bar in his pocket.

Chapter 33

Brian arrived minutes later together with a police van and a collection of armed men.

"Don't trust him further than you can throw him," Pete ordered, watching his quarry being levered from the bed.

"He's a rat and there's nothing worse than a cornered one," he added.

Brian grinned at him and Oliver, who had been attempting to do up his trousers with one hand, the other being completely useless, snarled at both of them.

"I want a doctor, look what that filthy mutt did to my hand; I could die. And …" he added, "I don't expect he even bothers to clean his teeth."

Brian looked at the damaged hand and sighed.

"I'll get the police doctor to look at it in the custody suite."

Oliver had the distinct impression that the charm had finally run out, and shrugged.

The two police officers Brian had come with propelled him out of the room and down the stairs. Fion, who had been watching at a safe distance with her two children entered the bedroom and wanly smiled at them both.

"Thanks. Thank you so very much. And Mr Pickles,

I think you are the smartest, bestest dog in the world." Mr Pickles loped towards her and sat at her feet and licked her hand, at which she threw her arms around him and gave him a loving, long hug.

"Does Mr Pickles like chocolate?" The eldest child asked, mesmerised.

"Oh he loves chocolate. Chocolate saved your mum you know," Pete replied.

"How?" asked the youngest who had her fingers in her mouth.

"Because the bad man had a Mars Bar in his pocket and when we were checking the garage Mr Pickles went all quiet and realised that there was an intruder and so he followed his scent all the way to your mummy's bedroom."

"Daddy was the bad man," the eldest stated.

"Yes." Pete answered.

"We know," the youngest nodded sagely.

"We've known for ever," the eldest grimly agreed.

"You did?" Their mother asked, surprised.

"Yes." Both children nodded. "Daddy didn't like us."

"Why on earth didn't you say?" their mother asked.

"Because he said he would really hurt us if we did," the eldest replied while the youngest nodded in agreement.

Fion, shocked, held out her arms and enveloped both her children, kissing both as if at any moment they would disappear.

"I'm so, so sorry," she cried, gulping back yet more tears.

Mr Pickles watched and then sat on his hind legs and howled.

"Wait there," the eldest ordered and ran from the room reappearing minutes later with an enormous bar of Cadbury's chocolate, which was then reverently laid at the stunned hound's feet.

"It's a chocolate monster bar, I got for my birthday and I've been saving it for a special day. And as Mr Pickles is special I think he should have it. It's got 144 pieces, 'cos I counted," he added.

Mr Pickles looked from the child to Pete and back again.

"You deserve it, but," Pete picked the bar up and held it gently, "you can have it a little bit at a time as a special treat."

Mr Pickles looked from the bar to the child and then to his master and back at the bar and suddenly rolled onto his back, thrust all four legs in the air and closed his eyes in an expression of divine doggy ecstasy.

The children both laughed delightedly and after Mr Pickles had rolled back with his tongue hanging out screamed in unison. "Make him do it again, again, again."

***

At the same time their father on reaching the waiting van, clutched his stomach and fell to the ground.

The men around him momentarily dropped their guard and he arose holding something black and shiny in his one good hand. In horror Brian watched as he raised the round object to his mouth and removed the pin on the handle.

Oliver Mandrake smiled and dropped the pin on the ground.

"I'm not going in there, I'd rather die." And in the shocked silence that followed dropped the grenade and ran. He was still running when it exploded. Glass shattered and the van blew backwards into the shrubbery surrounding the house. The police who had dived for cover emerged glass sparkling from their uniforms, their faces and hands bleeding from small cuts. Brian, his ears still ringing from the blast, clenched his fists in frustrated fury and shouted, "Don't just stand there, get after him, and you near the door – go up and get Mr Pickles."

Later as they scoured the countryside, Mr Pickles led them down to the small cove below the house and they looked in dismay at the empty floating pontoon to which, according to Fion, a small but fast motor boat had been attached.

"There's a really bad storm coming in from the south east," one of Brian's constables advised, looking out at the low blue-black clouds boiling up on the distant horizon.

"Good," Brian barked. "With any luck the little sod will drown."

"I wouldn't bank on it," Pete muttered as they stood side by side and watched Mr Pickles sit at the edge of the beach and howl.

Chapter 34

Bob answered the mobile and listened, a selection of emotions crossed his features and then with a sigh he mumbled, "Yes I'll tell them."

"What?" Tavistock and Clara asked, leaning in towards him and dreading the news until Bob sat back and smiled beautifully at them both.

"Fion is safe. Pete and Mr Pickles hadn't gone home because Mr Pickles came across the scent of something and tracked Oliver Mandrake into the house, up the stairs and into the bedroom before he could kill his wife."

"You mean he remembered Oliver Mandrake's scent," Tavistock asked incredulously.

"No, better than that, a bar of chocolate he had stashed in his pocket. According to his wife her husband always carried something around with him as he had a mild form of diabetes and a very sweet tooth."

"And she's okay?" Tavistock reiterated.

"Apart from a small wound on her neck and quite a bit of bruising, yes."

"Well all's well that ends well," Clara stated picking up the bottle and refilling his glass.

"Not exactly," Bob muttered with a frown.

"It appears that when they were just about to get him into the van, he produced a hand grenade – God alone knows where he got that from – he then pulled out the pin with his teeth and in the confusion managed to escape in a small boat they keep at the bottom of the garden. There is a storm brewing and he may drown or run out of fuel but …"

"But?" Tavistock repeated, as he got up and walked over to the window.

"But that wretched man has more lives than a cat so I don't hold out any hope that he will."

Clara looked down at the glass in her hand and while Tavistock stared at Bob she picked up the box containing the razor and smiled a small and secret smile.

Later after Bob had gone, picked up by his wife en route from her bridge club and Tavistock had told her husband that she would be staying overnight with Clara as she couldn't drive home, Clara stoked up the ailing fire and motioning Tavistock to sit, carefully opened the box, unwrapped the razor from the soft folds of leather surrounding it and handed it to her friend with the words, "You once asked me why it had stopped."

Tavistock nodded and looked down in puzzlement at the knife.

"Hold it and find out," Clara urged.

Tavistock picked it up and as she did so heard from a long way away the tuneless humming of an old music hall song.

Jack stood behind his master and carefully applied the shaving foam to the Ripper's face.

"Did you see the papers this morning?" Jack was asked. "The *Illustrated Police News* even have a cartoon about us. Fame at last, eh Jack?"

"Yes Sir," Jack muttered sharpening the razor on a long leather strop.

Their eyes met in the mirror, blue against brown and

then the blue eyes opened wide with shock as the razor sliced cleanly and quickly into his neck severing the carotid artery in less than the seconds it took him to understand what was happening.

As the life faded with the blood spurting from the mortal wound in his throat the Ripper could only stare as his killer calmly watched him die.

"And the name is John. John Arthur Kelly Callister. John after my father and Kelly from my mother's side. Kelly from the Isle of Man."

Afterwards as he carefully wrapped the dead man's fingers around the knife and after checking the scene and ensuring that all trace of the shaving foam had been removed he walked over to the door and before opening it, turned towards Tavistock and smiled, a smile that held such sadness in it that Tavistock moved towards him, only to be checked by an upturned hand.

"No, don't," the man she still thought of as Jack, ordered.

"I loved him, looked after him since he was small and God help me, covered up all his little crimes, the bigger ones too," he added ruefully, looking back at the body.

"But killing Nan, Nan who loved him. You know what he told me?" Jack swallowed and then as if pulling himself together clenched both hands into tight fists.

"He told me he killed all of them not to pass his anatomy exam, but to hide the one murder he needed to do. To kill the one woman who could stop his marriage. Told me her family would never forgive a liaison with a common little nurse from a small farming family. And tenant farmers at that. Common, my little Nan, common. And the sad thing is that she would never have told, never. She would have had the child, brought it up on her own and never breathed a word, nor asked for a penny either. She was that proud."

Tavistock nodded.

"And now what will you do?"" she asked.

"Do? I'm going to rouse the house and get the constable, tell them that he and Nan were lovers and that he was so distraught at the news of her murder that he killed himself. Doubtless the family will then throw money at the problem and hush it all up, like they always do."

"And then?"

"Then I'll go back home, home to my Blanche and a small cottage up in the hills, take my pension and keep sheep."

He sighed and then asked almost as an afterthought, "And you did get him didn't you? You got the pretender?"

"No, nearly. But we stopped him killing the last three."

"And the woman he said he loved?"

"Saved by a hound from hell."

He smiled at that and then moved towards her and putting a hand on her shoulder whispered, "Tell Clara, if she made a bargain with *him* she should use it."

Tavistock looked at him in a puzzled way until with a smile he let her go, walked a step towards the door and opened it. "You'd better go," he whispered.

"Thank you," Tavistock replied as the room faded away, to be replaced by the glow of Clara's invigorated fire.

"So what did he say?" Clara asked.

Tavistock wrinkled her nose in concentration. "He said ... Tell Clara that if she made a bargain with 'him' she should use it."

Clara sat back, a strange smile playing around her mouth. She then gently removed the knife from Tavistock's hands and after carefully rewrapping it, placed it back in its box and pushed down the lid.

"What did he mean, Clara?" Tavistock demanded, watching her intently.

"I have no idea," Clara replied, and Tavistock, realising that she was lying to the teeth and also that she would never tell, left it at that and yawningly demanded the use of the bathroom and a bed.

Chapter 35

Weeks later Clara and Mannanan sat in his office while Barty bustled around making the tea.

"He's definitely gone then?" Clara asked with a frown.

"Definitely. I'll know of course if he ever returns but I doubt if he will," Mannanan replied.

Clara bit her lip and then in frustration exclaimed,"How the hell do I track him down now?"

Mannanan shook his head and sighed and Clara picked up her teacup and angrily sipped at the potent brew.

"Um ... if I can be of assistance?" Barty murmured uncertainly behind them.

"What?" Mannanan and Clara asked in perfect unison.

Barty smiled and handed them a small piece of paper.

"What's this?" Mannanan demanded.

"It's his new address, the place he bought in the Canary Islands. The one that no one can find anything about because he paid cash and deleted all the files."

"Then how?"

"I went through all the files and information and apart from having a thing about chocolate, Oliver Mandrake also liked to gamble. Actually *like* is a bit weak really, our Wally loved to gamble and he still does. I've managed to track him down through the Poker Stars server and followed him down the line until I pop up in his house in his lounge overlooking the sea. There he is, large as life and twice as ugly engaged in the pursuit of pleasure, which was a good reason for leaving early and going and having a look outside to see where he was. Luckily it had a name on the gates and a roadsign opposite."

"You went down the line?" Mannanan asked in frank astonishment.

"Yeah."

"Can you do that? Can he do that?" Clara asked, unfolding the paper note and looking at the address.

"Yes he can, and yes he did," Mannanan exclaimed, getting up and patting Barty West on the back.

"Well I never," Clara declared before adding a heartfelt "Well done that man."

"Well done indeed," Mannanan agreed.

"Barty, take the day off, in fact you can take the week off!"

***

Oliver Mandrake extracted a solid gold krugerrand from the tube purporting to contain the best in Belgium chocolate and weighed it in his hand. He was about to replace it in the safe when the intercom on the gate bleeped at him.

"What is it?" he asked, applying his finger to the speak button.

"Package for Senor Gomez," came the bored reply.

"Leave it at the gate," he replied.

"I'm sorry Senor, but it says 'ere that it 'as to be signed for."

"Who sent it?"

"Um Singer and ..."

"Ah, that package. I'll buzz you in," he called, grabbing

the white towelling robe which hung on the back of a leather armchair.

As he stepped outside he could clearly see a capped slight figure staring into the depths of his pool.

"Well where is it?" he demanded.

"Here, Senor."

He grabbed the package and the clipboard that the courier wearing the FedEx cap and insignia was holding in one hand.

"Where do you want me to sign?" he asked.

The courier handed him a pen and pointed. "Here and here."

Oliver turned and as he did the courier slipped something from a pocket and taking him completely by surprise, swiftly cut his neck open from ear to ear, and then pushed him into the pool.

Oliver looked up as he clutched at his neck, vainly trying to stem the flow of blood which was gradually turning the clear water in the blue pool to a soft shade of rose.

Clara stood at the pool edge and removing her cap grinned down at him.

"For my Thomas," she advised him and then without a backwards glance she turned and walked away.

***

A few days later Bob and Brian sat again in Coffee Republic and watched the passers-by struggling gamely against a piercing wind and gusty shower of rain.

"Found in his own pool," Brian remarked, dipping a long almond biscotti into his mug.

"Really?"

"Yes, and with his throat cut."

"Apt."

"I thought so. Apparently they tracked him down through the fingerprints we had on file."

"Couldn't happen to a nicer chap."

"How did the … er … vermin exterminator, for want of a better word, get in?"

"Apparently the courier was approached by a woman with attributes who said she wanted to surprise her lover and paid him a small fortune to borrow his cap, jacket, clipboard and package."

"Clever."

"A woman, eh?"

"Hell hath no fury and all that."

"Any other clues?"

"None."

"What a shame."

They both grinned at each other and then happily turned to stare at the soaked and scurrying shoppers and office workers, safe in the knowledge that the one that had got away, hadn't.